ABOUT THE AUTHOR

George G. Gilman was born in 1936 in what was then a small village east of London. He attended local schools until the age of fifteen. Upon leaving school he abandoned all earlier ambitions and decided to become a professional writer, with strong leanings towards the mystery novel. He wrote short stories and books during evenings, lunch hours, at weekends, and on the time of various employers while he worked for an international newsagency, a film company, a weekly book-trade magazine and the Royal Air Force.

His first short (love) story was published when he was sixteen and the first (mystery) novel ten years later. He has been a full-time writer since 1970, writing mostly Westerns which have been translated into a dozen languages and have sold in excess of 16 million copies. He is married and lives on the Dorset coast, which is as far west as he intends to move right now.

GOING BACK

George G. Gilman

NEW ENGLISH LIBRARY
Hodder and Stoughton

for:
Jan Stuckey,
who finally made
it out west.

A New English Library
Original Publication, 1989

First New English Library
Paperback Edition 1989

British Library C.I.P.

Gilman, George G., *1936–*
  Going back.
  Rn: Terry Harknett
  I. Title
  II. Series
  823'.914[F]

ISBN 0-450-48775-X

Printed and bound in Great
Britain for Hodder and Stoughton
Paperbacks, a division of Hodder
and Stoughton Ltd., Mill Road,
Dunton Green, Sevenoaks, Kent
TN13 2YA (Editorial Office: 47
Bedford Square, London, WC1B
3DP) by Cox & Wyman Ltd.,
Reading, Berks.

AUTHOR'S NOTE

When the Edge series was thirty-three titles old I complied with requests from a considerable number of readers to write a collection of short stories which filled in some of the gaps in the half-breed's life: periods before the series began and between the endings of some books and the openings of others when what happened in the interim was not always fully explained at the time.

This book, entitled 'A Ride in the Sun', took the form of a running contemporary story interspersed with incidents from Edge's past. And the short story concept, along with the manner in which it was presented, proved so popular with Edge fans that I was persuaded to return to it, with a second collection of short stories within a longer one: 'The Moving Cage'.

This second collection also served another purpose: it enabled me to bring to a wider audience some Edge stories which had previously been published in magazines.

The book you now hold is the third collection of George G. Gilman short stories. But these, of course, relate incidents from the past of Adam Steele, cut into a contemporary account of the Virginian's life since he put down roots in California's Providence River Valley.

Just one story, 'The Troublemakers' has been published before: as 'Bad Business at Newville' in the January 1981 edition of the late lamented *Western Magazine*.

As in 'A Ride in the Sun' and 'The Moving Cage', a brief introduction to each story explains precisely when these incidents took place in the context of the entire Adam Steele series.

1

Throughout his life of something over forty but not yet fifty years, Adam Steele had at times gotten the reputation for being a tightwad. But whenever he gave consideration to what other people thought about him in this respect, he preferred to think of it as being careful with money. Certainly he detested seeing it wasted.

Which was why he was riding in a creaking and juddering Concord coach of the San Francisco and Central California Stage Line. Enduring the discomforts of the journey and not enjoying the company of his fellow passengers, instead of being astride a saddled horse, setting his own pace. The target of the flirtatious attentions of a homely young woman and of the resentment of her downright ugly mother, and the cause of amusement to a married couple of middle years and an elderly drummer.

Trouble was, Steele had bought a round trip ticket between Providence and San Francisco. And the SF&CC Stage Line Company did not make refunds for portions of a journey paid for and not travelled. So, having experienced the discomforts of the northward trip—when the jolting and dusty ride in another ancient and poorly maintained stage had been made worse by the company of two spoiled children and their weak-willed parents, then a talkative drunk and next a man with a large dog that had fleas and smelled bad—Steele had not been about to surrender the ride back home. Which would involve him in the additional expense of purchasing a horse and gear.

Even though as a horse breeder he knew he could certainly buy a good mount at a reasonable price in San Francisco and sell the animal at a profit in the Providence River Valley. The stage line company would still have his money for the return half of the trip he did not take. Which he could not allow. Because he was careful with his money, hated to waste it. Some people would say he was a tightwad with it.

'You know somethin' Mr Steele?' Belle Cowley asked pensively.

The Virginian looked at the plain young woman who sat facing him in the right hand corner of the seat, her back to the way they were travelling. Knew that if she had not been quite so homely he would have welcomed how she broke in on his train of thought: for he did not enjoy reflecting on the less than flattering aspects of his character. And he certainly did not like admitting that since he had started to lead the settled life of a horse rancher it sometimes mattered what people thought of him and his ways.

He replied to the woman: 'I know I should think about changing some of my ways, Miss Cowley.'

She dismissed the incomprehensible response with a shake of her head, told him: 'I know I think you've got the kind of face that's better suited to bein' clean shaven.'

'You mind your own business, young lady!' Thelma Cowley censured her daughter. She sat beside Belle so was well placed to glare resentfully at Steele: which she did often, tacitly blaming him for the need to reproach her daughter.

Belle, who was in her mid-twenties, skinny-framed and thin-faced, had pale eyes that were too small, crooked teeth, stringy brown hair and a bad skin. She shrugged her narrow shoulders and turned her head to peer out through the dusty window at the wooded mountainscape across which they were rattling. While she did this, she directed a lascivious wink at Steele. Which her mother failed to see.

Mrs Thelma Cowley, who had formally introduced herself and her daughter when they boarded at the Possum River Way Station an hour earlier, showed Steele another glowering look before she once more bent her head to peer longsightedly down over her ample bosom to read from the large Bible on her lap. Probably she seemed heavier than she was in relation to her sparsley built daughter, and *vice versa*. But, the smallness and the washed out colour of her eyes and her crooked teeth, if nothing else, proved clear evidence of their close family relationship.

Both Cowley women were garbed in homespun dresses that had seen better days, been laundered until the colourings faded, and darned so often that the mismatched yarns of the repairs

10

looked like features of the garments' design.

They were not ashamed of their poverty, which was fine with Steele, who had been very rich and very poor: had learned it served no useful purpose to be proud of possessions or disgraced by the lack of them.

Unlike the Cowleys, he did not generally reveal his feelings about anything. And had become an even tempered man for most of the time. Learned along many dangerous trails that it was safer to seem to be so when circumstances triggered heated emotions toward people who created the disconcerting situations.

The mostly grey beard, slightly tinged with red, to which Belle Cowley had referred, helped him to appear at ease when he was feeling the very opposite. For the way it straggled around his mouth, the beard concealed the set of his lips and allowed him to compress them in front of gritted teeth while he concentrated on keeping the fires of anger, or hatred, or lust, or the urge to kill, out of his coal-black eyes.

Now it was merely mild irritation he sought to hide as George Rutherford and the Townsends enjoyed the way Belle Cowley baited him and her mother held him responsible for encouraging her.

Or maybe he just imagined that this trio of passengers saw him as the butt of a running joke that amused them. Perhaps he was desperate to denounce anyone but himself for allowing the situation to develop: letting the Cowleys get to him the way they were. It sure wouldn't have happened in the old days, before he took the considered decision to become like . . .

'My goodness, a person would think they'd do something to improve the comfort of public transport!' Delores Townsend complained shrilly as the Virginian's thoughts started along another unwelcome line.

The woman spoke as the stage lurched violently to the side and she was pressed heavily against Steele: hurriedly straightened up, wriggled back along the seat to open a gap between herself and him: crunched herself tight against her husband.

Mrs Townsend had made her disapproval of Steele known from the outset of the trip—she and her husband Alvin had boarded the stage at the San Francisco depot, been forced to

11

share the same forward-facing seat as him because the opposite three were occupied by Rutherford and two younger salesmen who had gotten off the stage at the stop before the Cowleys boarded at the Possum River Way Station.

Shortly after the Concord rolled out of the city depot, the statuesque and grey haired Mrs Townsend, bright eyed, heavily bejewelled and strongly perfumed, had asked Steele if it was strictly necessary that he ride the stage with a rifle wedged between his right leg and the door.

He replied politely, though maybe a little curtly, that it certainly was necessary: and knew she would have pursued the point with something akin to bristling anger had not her slightly taller and much heavier husband, bald headed, wax moustached and business suited, advised her against it, his voice a rasping whisper that only she heard clearly.

Then Rutherford, obsequious mannered, grey haired, and grey faced, had attempted to strike up a placating conversation: commented on the unusual kind of rifle it was, not the universal Winchester repeater which most men who bore arms carried if they considered a revolver was not sufficient protection.

In the same mild-mannered but less than encouraging tone with which he responded to Mrs Townsend, Steele pointed out he did not carry a revolver: and told his fellow passengers the rifle was a relatively rare Colt Hartford revolver action model to which he was sentimentally attached.

Because of how he successfully checked attempted conversation at the commencement of the trip, Steele had only to contend with the physical discomforts of the ride and the less than friendly attitudes of the other passengers toward him: until the Cowley mother and daughter boarded. Introduced themselves and insisted upon shaking hands with everyone. And then Belle, who looked not at all like his idea of a vamp, began to flirt with the Virginian with pointed remarks and unmistakable expressions. Which caused her mother frequently to interrupt her devout Bible study. Both of them sorely trying Steele's patience.

'You are perfectly correct, madam,' Rutherford agreed eagerly with Mrs Townsend. 'I travel many hundreds of miles by stage each month in the course of my business. And I never cease to be amazed when I reach the end of such trips with no

12

bones broken.'

'I consider it's lucky for the wife and me that we have such little cause to travel,' Alvin Townsend put in quickly, as anxious as the salesman to sustain the exchange of small talk. As if they were unnerved by long absences of spoken words within the Concord as it swayed and rattled and creaked behind the labouring six horse team which moved at a straining walk up a gentle but lengthy, curving grade.

'Lucky is what you are, I can tell you that.'

'We wouldn't be doing so now, except our daughter in Bending will shortly deliver our first grandchild.'

Concern about the disconcerting atmosphere within the stage was forgotten as Townsend beamed and his wife exuded pride in the time-honoured fashion of potential grandparents about to be assured that the family bloodline will be continued for at least one more generation.

But George Rutherford was disgruntled by the revelation. Probably on his many stage trips he had been bored too often by fellow passengers enthusing about passions in which he had no interest. He nodded, grunted, immediately returned to the subject which had gotten the conversation started.

'Of course, the railroad is by far the most comfortable way to travel overland. The permanent way is so much smoother than these Godawful trails the stages have to——'

'God made nothin' that is awful, Mr Rutherford!' Thelma Cowley interrupted grimly, stabbed a finger at the large Bible open on her lap so that she would not lose her place as she raised her head, turned to glare at the startled hardware salesman beside her. 'It is what mankind chooses to do to the beautiful world the Almighty created that so often finishes in ugliness.'

Rutherford gulped in surprise at the woman's vehemence, then looked chastened as he muttered: 'Quite so, madam. It was not my intention to give offence.'

Mrs Cowley vented a throat-clearing sound of qualified acceptance of the drummer's implied apology, and returned to her Bible study.

Rutherford hurried on before Townsend took the opportunity to change the subject again: 'Of course, the basic Concord coach was never built for our rutted Western trails.

They're manufactured in the East, you know? Plainly they were intended to be used on town streets back there. And on the smoother turnpikes of New England. Just building them bigger and strengthening the springs a little has hardly been sufficient to suit them to our Western purposes.'

A front wheel found another hole in the trail and the stage lurched in the opposite direction. Steele braced himself from being thrown against Mrs Townsend as she complained through clenched teeth:

'The least they could do is provide decently padded upholstery!'

Then she vented a small cry of anger and perhaps of pain as the front and rear wheels jolted across an extensive area of uneven trail.

'I gotta agree with you on that, lady,' Belle Cowley growled, turned her head sharply away from her baleful survey of the passing scene beyond the window.

Steele did not believe it was an accident that the daughter's bony elbow dug into the fleshy side of her mother. This as her small eyes brightened and she showed her crooked teeth in a meaningful grin which she directed at Steele when she added:

'It's at times like these I get jealous of my Ma: how she has so much extra padding that takes the sting outta most of these bumps.'

'I told you before, Belle!' Thelma Cowley snapped without looking up from the Bible. 'Don't you be so personal about folks! Even your own mother, girl.'

'Mind you,' Belle went on, her coquettish gaze fixed firmly on Steele's impassive face, 'I reckon for most of the time it's best a woman ain't too well padded. If she's aimin' to catch the eye of the men. Ain't that right, Mr Steele?'

'I wouldn't know about other men, ma'am,' the Virginian replied. And glanced at Thelma Cowley, expecting to hear her rebuke Belle again for this latest foray into the forbidden territory of sexual innuendo.

But it seemed she was too deeply engrossed in a particular passage of the Bible: followed the printed words with a moving finger across the page as she continued to keep her head bent forward.

'Well, I know about the ones I've been friendly with,' Belle

14

answered emphatically. 'And I reckon if a girl wants to look good to most men, she can have too much of what makes her different from a man.'

She pulled back her shoulders and arched her back, to give more prominence to the small mounds of her breasts.

Mrs Cowley suddenly turned the page noisily, in a gesture of anger at what she had heard.

Delores Townsend rasped: 'Oh, my goodness.'

Her husband gulped.

George Rutherford groaned: 'Oh no, not again, God-damnit!'

Thelma Cowley reminded grimly: 'Sir, I've already made it clear I object to the takin' of the Lord's name in vain.'

As Steele saw the lascivious smile on Belle's face deliberately change into a grin of enjoyment, he became aware that the Townsends and Rutherford had not vented their shocked responses to the woman's brazen words and gestures. And now he looked at the older Cowley woman, saw the stern tone of her voice was emphasised by the icy look in her flesh-crowded eyes which fixed their unblinking gaze on him rather than the man she had censured. In her right she held a brass-framed Colt Deringer which was no longer than five inches from the rear of the bird-beak butt in her fist to the barrel muzzle that was aimed at Steele's chest. Her left hand continued to hold open the Bible: as if purposely to show where more that half its pages had been carefully cut to form a hollow in which the tiny, single shot gun could be concealed.

'You, sir,' Mrs Cowley went on, pushing the small weapon an inch closer to its target, 'will allow my daughter to have that fancy rifle of yours. My pistol does not look so dangerous, I know. But I can assure you that at this distance it can kill you.'

Steele moved his leg slightly to the side, signalled with a nod that the young woman opposite should reach across the aisle and remove the Colt Hartford. He said evenly to Thelma Cowley: 'I like to think I do my best to live by what's in the Good Book, ma'am.'

Either the driver or the guard said something that did not reach clearly into the Concord against the sounds of its slow uphill progress. The second man replied more distinctly:

'Yeah, Ezra, I see 'em.' He sounded wearily resigned to an

inevitable outcome to what was getting started.

'This is the third time in a year I've been on a stage that was held up,' George Rutherford complained. Which explained why he had said what he did when he saw Thelma Cowley take the gun out of the Bible.

Mrs Townsend raised a hand to her throat, clutched at the three ropes of pearls that encircled her wrinkled neck. Then she recalled that she wore bejewelled rings on three fingers of each hand. And she dragged the hand away from her throat, linked it with the other on her lap and endeavoured to clasp them together so the jewellery did not show.

'If nobody does anythin' stupid, then nobody's gonna get hurt in any way,' Thelma Cowley promised, her tone of voice less hard than before while her cold-eyed gaze darted from where her daughter fisted a bony hand around the barrel of the Colt Hartford and dragged the rifle across the aisle, to glance at Steele, then the Townsends, Rutherford: the Virginian again. 'Hurtin' folks don't put bread on the table, right?'

George Rutherford and Alvin Townsend nodded vigorously. Dolores Townsend tried to say something, but needed to clear her throat noisily before she was able to rasp:

'Nobody here will try to prevent you doing what you want, I'm sure.'

She peered pleadingly around at her fellow passengers, gasped when Ezra called down from the outside seat:

'I have to tell you folks we're bein' held up. Three men at the top of this rise have got rifles levelled at me and Steve.'

Steele knew from overhearing talk at the San Francisco depot that Ezra was the middle-aged, lean-framed and dour-faced driver of the stage: Steve was the slightly younger, much more beefily built guard, with a quick smile.

'There's two women inside here got guns can kill your passengers, driver!' Belle answered, happily triumphant.

What she said was true in essence, but the way she continued to hold the Colt Hartford around the muzzle end of the barrel, butt resting on the floor of the stage, meant the rifle posed no immediate threat. Which did not matter too much right then. For there was unwavering determination in the expression and attitude of her mother as she kept the tiny handgun aimed at the centre of Steele's chest.

16

This dissuaded the Virginian from contemplating any move against the Cowley women and their male partners in crime at the top of the rise. And, irrespective of how they felt about him, Steele was sure the Townsends and Rutherford would not deliberately do anything that might result in his death weighing on their conscience.

Ezra yelled: 'Okay, you guys! We won't give you no trouble!'

Steve shouted louder: 'Right, we know you've got some help aboard!'

'That's real smart!' a man roared from along the trail, probably no more than two hundred feet or so. 'You rein in that team right about now!'

Ezra barked a command at the horses in the traces and the brake blocks squeaked on the wheelrims.

Belle Cowley, a wide grin of greed now showing more of her misshapen teeth and squeezing her tiny eyes to gleaming slits, said to Mrs Townsend: 'And you'll be smart, lady, if you don't take Ma and me for chumps.'

The well-dressed, richly-jewelled woman vented a low-toned gasp. And the sweat of fear caused her perfume to smell cloyingly sweet. She started to splutter: 'I'm afraid I don't——'

Belle snorted, cut in: 'You don't really think Ma and me ain't seen them pretty rings you got on your fingers? So why don't you start to take 'em off instead of tryin' to hide them after we been seein' them for better than an hour already?'

Mrs Townsend shuddered and her husband rested a hand ineffectually on her arm.

Thelma Cowley instructed flatly: 'And when you got the rings off, you can unfasten that pearl necklace. You gents, we'll be takin' whatever kind of rings and watches and such like you happen to be wearin'. Along with cash money.'

'But we don't want it right now!' Bella snarled tautly when Alvin Townsend pushed his free hand inside his suit jacket. 'We don't want no hands goin' outta sight into no pockets until we're all outta this rig and the boys got their guns coverin' you!'

The Concord jolted to a halt and Belle Cowley vented a sigh of either relief or satisfaction.

Her mother jerked her head toward the door of the left hand side, ordered: 'Everyone out that way. You first, Mr Rutherford. Then Mr Townsend. I know from your accent that you're from the south, Mr Steele. But you'll have to forget them Southern gentlemen ways for awhile. Because us ladies are gonna be last out. Be a bad mistake if anyone took exception to that.'

Steele said evenly: 'I reckon I stopped being a gentleman about the first time a lady held a gun on me, ma'am.'

He needed to continue to work at presenting the outward appearance that he was calmly at ease in the tense, summer-heated, strongly-perfumed interior of the stage. While behind this façade he was bowstring taut: angry at the people pulling the hold-up, and at himself for failing to notice any signs there was something wrong about the Bible-studying mother and her shameless daughter. He was convinced he should have spotted that while one pretended such devout interest in the Bible, she was just waiting for a signal from the other that the time was right to take the gun from out of its mutilated pages.

But as yet none of the tension that had built so steadily within him was channelled toward looking for a chance to make a counter move. Not within the confines of the rig, with three rifle-toting men close by outside. Not until Ezra, the driver, rasped at Steve, riding shotgun:

'Don't be a crazy fool!'

Then, as the Cowley mother looked at her daughter, in the stretched second while their frightened gazes were locked, Steele came to within a hairsbreadth of grasping one of the options available to him. None of them had anything but a long chance of letting him survive, but he was prepared to accept the risk if the alternative was to die because of other people's panic.

He could reach through the slit in the outside seam of his right pants leg, draw the knife carried in a boot sheath. Or power forward, wrench the tiny pistol out of the woman's grasp. If necessary, kill one or both Cowley women. Or use the threat of death to get back the Colt Hartford. Which he had to do to have a chance of dealing with the three men he could hear riding their horses at a walk down from the crest of the hill toward the stalled Concord.

Then the horses were reined to a halt and there was a moment of silence. A fusillade of rifle shots that sounded shockingly loud.

The two Cowley women unlocked their gazes, and Thelma

thrust the Deringer another inch closer to Steele. Her daughter mouthed a curse and made to unlatch the door.

Outside a man screamed in agony.

Inside Delores Townsend tried to scream in terror, but managed only a sound something like a choked cough.

The powerfully built guard, who had been sitting at the right hand end of the outside seat, fell backwards across the roof luggage, then toppled sideways. His bloodstained clothing and bullet-shattered head were clear to see as he dropped past the window of the door which Belle had been about to open.

'Shit, Ma, they done killed him!' she rasped.

'Girl, you got no call to use that kinda talk!' her mother snarled.

And Steele, at the centre of the ugly woman's hard-eyed attention, knew she could see through his unruffled exterior. He knew, too, her attitude was in no degree deceptive: Thelma Cowley would not hesitate to blast a killing shot at him if he made one move she mistrusted.

'It was just him!' Ezra pleaded, pain or fear or a combination of both squeezing his throat so the words emerged as a rasping whisper. 'I wasn't gonna——'

A single rifle shot sounded strangely low key in the wake of the barrage moments before. But the lone bullet had the awesome effect of ending the life of a man. The driver's slight form thudded hard against the roof of the stage. But the impetus of just one bullet driving into his flesh failed to tip him off the Concord to the ground like the guard.

'That's two, the trigger happy fools!' Thelma snarled.

She spoke out of the side of her mouth, her lips hardly moving in front of her crooked teeth, while her threatening stare continued to be fixed on Steele. Then her eyes suddenly widened, to express something akin to pleading: like she knew she had done all she could to convince him she would do whatever was necessary, now implored him not to do anything to force her into squeezing the trigger of the tiny gun.

'Everythin' all right in there, Mrs Cowley?' a man called against the sounds of repeater rifle actions being pumped, the scrape of slow-moving hooves on hard-packed ground.

'Smooth as silk and sweet as molasses, Daryl!' Belle blurted eagerly. And from yet another change in the shape of her smile,

19

Steele thought it likely Daryl was one of the men she had known who currently rated higher than most.

'And not a drop of blood spilled in here!' her mother roared.

The harsh tone left no question that she did not approve of the double shooting. But then, as if she abruptly considered this might be seen as a sign of weakness by the other passengers, she glanced grimly around, felt confident enough to allow the aim of the gun to shift from Steele and direct its threat elsewhere as she added, low and meaningfully: 'Yet!'

'Okay, you guys, get outta the stage!' Belle urged, no longer intent on opening the right hand door now that the blood-run corpse of Steve was sprawled on the trail immediately outside. She made to get to her feet, using the Colt Hartford as a lever in the manner of a cane. But froze when her mother barked:

'Stay put, girl! I said gentlemen first.'

Now it was Thelma's turn to use a bent elbow, jabbed it into the side of Rutherford, unconcerned that the gun muzzle again swept away from the target of Steele's chest. For hooves had ceased to thud on the trail as the three mounts were reined to a halt in a line beside the Concord. Men and animals seen against a backdrop of the mountainscape of the Sierra Nevadas, featured with tree and rock outcrops, the distant highest ridges capped by year-long snow.

Each of the men held a levelled Winchester, with the hammer back, smoke no longer wisping from the muzzle. Two of the men smiled, the third scowled.

George Rutherford turned the door handle, then froze in the process of leaving the stage when he saw the three men, the three rifles aimed at his head over a range of ten feet or so.

'Step right on out, folks,' the eldest of the three invited cheerfully. Like the others, he was in his twenties. He had fiery red hair showing beneath the brim of his hat and in long sideburns, but his bushy moustache grew a mixture of blond and grey.

'Yes, indeed,' the second smiling man said. He was at the centre of the short line and was in the middle agewise. His complexion was dark hued, and there was about the shape of his features a suggestion that he had either Mexican or maybe Indian blood in his heritage. He was skinny enough to look undernourished, but in his face when he was smiling was a vitality that indicated he had more energy than his two associates together. 'Step outside and take a look at this big and beautiful world. But you keep it in mind you may never see it again if you do not do like you are told.'

Neither of these was Daryl. So the youngest one was: the shortest and the broadest, much of his bulk comprised of excess fat, from the way his shirt and pants bulged, strained their stitching. He had a round, smooth-skinned, clean-shaven, dull-eyed face that looked like it did not often spread with a smile.

All three were dressed in Western style work clothes and had gunbelts slung around their waists, revolver butts jutting out of tied-down holsters. Like their clothing, their weapons were far from new.

'You'll have no trouble from me,' Rutherford assured them as he slowly folded open the door, descended unhurriedly from the stage, his hands pushed forward and raised midway between his waist and his shoulders in token gesture of co-operative surrender.

'He says it's the third time in a year he's been held up,' Belle said as Alvin Townsend began to climb out of the stage when his wife gestured, angrily as well as fearfully, for him to let go of her arm and do so.

He almost stumbled on the steps when he looked over his shoulder, had his gaze drawn away from his wife inside the stage to the body of Ezra sprawled among the baggage on the roof.

'Have a good trip and come back next fall! the redhead with the blond moustache said gleefully, and giggled.

'Men are dead here, Ricky!' Thelma Cowley snapped, and made an ushering gesture with the Deringer at Steele. 'Save your childish jokes for a better time!'

When the Virginian stepped out of the Concord, blinked in the bright afternoon sunlight of the late summer day, the trio of confident young men paid him no more attention than they had to George Rutherford and Alvin Townsend. Obviously they did not, as Mrs Cowley had, see him as more dangerous than the other passengers.

Then Ricky and the dark-complexioned man broadened their grins of pleasure, and Daryl licked his lips with a brand of hunger as Delores Townsend stepped cautiously down from

21

the stage: perhaps on her guard against tripping like her husband, or maybe afraid she would faint.

In other circumstances, the reactions of the three young men might have been triggered by the statuesque form of the older woman and the elegance with which she moved. But in the here and now it was clearly the sparkling rings on her fingers and the richly-sheened pearls at her throat that aroused their interest. Along with the thought that if a woman wore such gems while she rode the stage, it was likely there were more and even better of the same in her luggage.

'It seems to me, Mrs Cowley,' Ricky said, his voice slightly husky, 'that better times are about to begin for us.'

Thelma now allowed herself a fleeting smile as she stepped down on to solid ground, saw that the trio of mounted men had her fellow passengers safely covered with the rifles and felt able to open the Bible, replace the tiny gun to its hiding place and snap the book firmly closed. Then she breathed a small sigh of satisfaction, allowed:

'Yes, indeed, boys. I do believe our troubles may be over.'

She waited until Belle had stepped down from the stage, still using the Colt Hartford like a walking cane, before she added with a shake of her head: 'But I do so wish it could have been achieved without bloodshed.'

'It couldn't be helped, Mrs Cowley,' Daryl said sullenly, refusing to meet the eager gaze of Belle.

'That's right,' Ricky agreed, shot an expectant glance at the dark-complexioned man beside him. 'Mel?'

'That sure is right, Mrs Cowley,' he supplied, nodded his head rapidly. Then he glanced up at Ezra's body sprawled across the roof of the Concord, crouched in the saddle to peer beneath the stage where the other corpse lay. 'Them or us it was. There just wasn't no help for it, honest, Mrs Cowley.'

'Okay, okay!' Belle muttered sulkily, glared at Mel, then Daryl, finally at the group of four prisoners before she demanded: 'Let's stop wastin' time and get on with this!'

Steele drawled: 'Don't yell at us, lady. It's not us holding you up.'

The Betrayal

Toward the end of STEELE'S WAR PART TWO in the book entitled *The Preacher*, there is a five month period in the summer of 1862 when Lieutenant Adam Steele of the CSA cavalry disguises himself as a civilian to evade capture by the Yankees as he strives to rejoin the Rebel army. This episode took place during that time.

The Virginian was feeling low on the storm-filled night he found shelter in the rambling, abandoned house, now fallen into disrepair, which stood on the eastern slopes of the Blue Ridge Mountains of North Carolina. He guessed about ten miles south of the town of Boone, where he had been told he might get a job driving a freight wagon on routes up into Virginia.

He was relieved to find the massive front door swung open easily at a light push. Grateful to discover the place was still partially furnished. Even more appreciative that in an upstairs room with an unbroken window there was a narrow bed; albeit stripped down to its bare springs.

With a mouldy-smelling rug serving as a makeshift mattress and his sodden duster for a cover, he was able to make himself more comfortable than on many past nights when circumstances had forced him to sleep a lot rougher than this. But he had some trouble getting to sleep in this big house on the thickly-wooded hillside. The rain beating on the roof and lashing at the windows and the intermittent thunder and lightning were at first the cause. But, too, as he waited for bone-deep weariness and the draining tension of dangerous travel to transcend these sounds of the storm, his mind was host to the experiences of the recent past. Since the fortunes of war had forced him to conceal his identity as a Confederate cavalry lieutenant.

At first he adopted the disguise of a preacher, but he quickly discovered he could not hope to sustain the lie of being a man of the cloth as he made his way out of Mississippi and across Tennessee: heading for North Carolina and ultimately his native Virginia. Where he would once more become a soldier.

It was at another abandoned house, much smaller than this one, close to Chattanooga, where he found an outfit of civilian clothing that made him look like an itinerant hand for hire. And he retained only the pair of eyeglasses which he had stolen along with the preacher's vestments, for they served to support his story that he was not as able-bodied as he seemed; was just too acutely short-sighted to be a soldier and fire a gun with any reasonable degree of accuracy.

He plotted and followed his course according to what he learned of the progress of the war. Sometimes what he read in newspapers, more often rumours picked up in conversation: when he was directly involved or was just an eavesdropper. In saloons, stores, on street corners, an occasional social.

He paid particular attention whenever he read or heard of the whereabouts, the successes and setbacks, of General Stonewall Jackson. For this was the man he intended to serve under. And because he possessed this burning ambition, at no time while he sought to achieve the aim did he consider himself a deserter.

Circumstances outside his control had separated him from his men. Stranded him in states that supported the secessionist cause but were occupied by superior numbers and better organised Union forces. Against which were ranged widely scattered, badly equipped bands of Rebels: like the one he had gotten attached to aboard the ironclad *Pride of Memphis* under the lunatic command of Major Garner.

Steele wanted no further part in that kind of war. He needed to serve under a fine commanding officer like Jackson. Be a good officer himself, primed to do his duty efficiently and honourably.

For he was just twenty-five, a rich Southern gentleman, and such ideals were important to him. Which was why he was living the lie, maintaining the pretence of being handicapped and unfit for military service as he did any work available that paid enough to feed him and finance his hazardous travels.

He did not often forget he was a soldier with a cause for which to fight, and sought whenever possible to hone his fighting skills. He had always been a crack shot with a rifle from his hunting days as a rich man's son. He had no rifle with him now, but he had acquired a knife he carried in a booth sheath. And a Navy Colt.

He practised with both weapons whenever he could. Mostly with the knife, for it could be thrown silently, made only a soft thud each time it struck, with increasing accuracy, whatever makeshift target he had fashioned. It was not so easy for a cavalry officer pretending to be a hired hand to fire the big Colt. Often because such practice would be sure to arouse suspicion. Also because he could not often afford to buy ammunition out of his invariably low pay.

Anyway, he never had—and was sure he could never acquire—the same aptitude for firing a pistol as he did for the rifle: he was a natural rifleman, his father's friends used to say when he was given his first weapon as a small child.

But would he ever get to use his natural ability with a rifle and his newly developed skill with a throwing knife against the Yankees? Who seemed to be winning every engagement in every theatre of the war.

He was growing impatient, but the going was tough through the mountains and he made slower progress than he intended after he left his last job as a store clerk two weeks ago. Once he had to call a complete halt for three days, eking out his meagre supplies to near starvation level while he endured a fever. As he sweated and shivered in the cave, he felt he came closer to death than at any time in any of the battles and skirmishes he had fought during the war.

Then this night, as the summer electric storm unleashed itself, a similar brand of depression threatened to drown him in sucking selfpity. Until he stumbled upon the big house and decided the door which opened so easily and the adequately furnished bedroom were signs his luck was going to change.

Which was maybe why he found his mind filled with so many memories of recent bad times while the lightning flashed, the thunder cracked and the rain sheeted: while he remained safe and warm and comfortable.

When sleep came it held him deep and secure for many untroubled hours, easing his mind and resting his body: soothing mental anguish and relieving physical aches. And just for an instant when he first woke, the bad times had been erased from his memory: so he thought of himself as Lieutenant Adam Steele, Confederate States of America cavalry officer. Bursting with youthful vigour and shining hope. Prepared to do whatever was asked of him to support the Cause in which he so fervently believed: win the glorious victory over the misguided Yankee armies of Abraham Lincoln.

But all this for just a brief fragment of time. Before he snapped open his eyes. Saw the surroundings of the decrepit bedroom, smelled the staleness of their decay, remembered where he was and why he was there. Heard a woman ask in a brightly eager tone:

'What do you think, Major Tremlett?'

Steele started to fold up on the bed. Froze when a spring creaked, sounding obtrusively loud in the silence from elsewhere. Thus did he realise not even the lightest of rain was falling against the drop-pebbled window beyond the foot of the bed, through which the light of an unsunny morning was shafting.

'What was that?' a man asked, startled.

'What, Major? Oh, you mean that creaking sound just now? Nothing to be concerned about. Old houses do creak and groan, you know. They talk, some fanciful people would have it. And after last night's rainstorm there are sure to be lots of timbers drying out here this morning. What do you think of the place?'

'It's in rather a bad state of disrepair,' the man answered immediately, like he had been convinced by the woman's explanation for the sound.

'Well, it has been standing empty since long before the war. Something like ten years, I should say. Do you know the story of why such a once fine house was left to rot this way?'

Steele eased carefully off the bed, paused each time the shifting of his slight weight caused the bed springs to protest again, a floorboard to creak. But Tremlett seemingly remained happy about sodden timbers drying out, for he did not interrupt the account he was being given about why the once fine house was abandoned all those years ago.

The Virginian had them placed in the entrance hall at the foot of the elegant stairway. The woman's voice continued to rise clearly up to where Steele made to leave the bedroom, moved gingerly toward the door that stood slightly ajar.

'Three elderly spinster sisters lived here. They inherited it from their father who was rich enough to leave them adequately provided for when he died. But they were not so rich as many believed when they died. Were murdered, in fact. Horribly tortured and murdered, Major. By two young men who thought, as many people did, that there was a great deal of money hidden in this house.

'The culprits were captured, tried and hanged for what they did. And I don't think many people came here afterwards. For the general opinion then was that the sisters were not so wealthy as everyone had believed. That they had just about spent out what their father left them before they were so brutally killed.'

Steele had brought the Navy Colt from the bed. Now thrust it under his belt at his belly as he eased the door open wider. Held his breath as he tried to recall if the hinges had creaked when he had opened the door to enter the room at the height of the storm. When he probably would not have heard it, damnit. Now he heard footfalls advancing up the stairs and he froze.

The woman talked on. 'There was nobody to inherit the house from the sisters. Nor debts to be met. And nobody wanted to live here after that horrible crime was committed. So it was left to rot.'

'Yes, I see.' He was starting to sound bored by the story.

'It was said that sometimes other men came to the place. To try to find the fortune those murderers couldn't. And children used to play here. Until a boy, one of several young mischief-makers, fell off the roof. Cracked open his skull on the porch steps out front.'

'That was tragic, Miss Marigold.' He did not sound shocked.

'Shortly after the accident, rumours began to circulate that the house was haunted by the ghost of that young boy. As far as I know, nobody has ever been here since. I'm sure no local people ever come near the place.'

Now Major Tremlett did speak with a degree of concern. 'We'll have to be careful with that tale of a haunting, Miss Marigold. The sort of people who'll be stopping at the house tend to be superstitious by nature, disturbed by such nonsense.'

'I realise that, Major!' she replied, and her voice suddenly sounded a little strained. Like she was finding it difficult to remain polite because she resented the man's implications that she had not considered the obvious. 'But it's surely not likely they will know of it. It's purely local nonsense and our visitors will come from much further afield. Be on their way again as soon as possible. And as I said, I'm sure no local people will come up to the house. Which makes it such a perfect place for our purposes.'

Steele left the door open some six inches, moved to the other side of it. And despite the danger of his situation he found himself intrigued by what the pair were talking about. Could make an educated guess what it was as he peered through the crack on the hinged side of the door: where he was well hidden but had a clear view of the man and woman as they reached the head of the stairway.

Miss Marigold was a stunningly beautiful blonde of thirty or so, elegantly dressed in pale blue to match her eyes. Her flawless skin was just lightly powdered. She was tall and slender, and if she had any fault at first impression it was that she had a studied aristocratic bearing: which was matched by her manner of speech when she thought the major had underestimated her intelligence.

Tremlett was a Union infantry officer. Ten years the woman's senior, he was a couple of inches taller than her, just as slimly built in a masculine way. He would probably be considered handsome by women of any age: he possessed that distinguished look that most men with prematurely silver hair can achieve quite naturally.

Steele had so far not been able to aspire to this, perhaps because his red hair had turned white at too early an age: before his nondescriptly handsome face had matured enough to complement the pale colour of his hair.

Not that he was thinking about his looks—which were haggard from the recent fever and not enough to eat for long weeks. This effect emphasised by the fact he had not shaved his

28

more red than grey bristles in several days.

He lowered his hand from where he had been chewing on the thumb knuckle, draped it over the butt of the revolver which was thrust into his belt at the belly.

'When will you be ready to take the first group?' the major asked as the woman moved slightly ahead of him, toward the partly open door behind which Steele waited.

Before the Virginian drew away, turned and put his back to the wall immediately alongside the door, he saw the distinguished face of the stiffly talking, staidly walking Tremlett alter expression. Show blatant lust as his gleaming grey eyes raced their hungry gaze up and down the long length of the woman's slender but emphatically curved body as soon as she stepped ahead of him, could not see this new brand of attention he paid her.

'Why, immediately,' she replied as she halted, pushed a hand forward to swing the door open wider.

It folded toward the Virginian, who clenched his first around the revolver butt, but did not draw it. His hand on the cold metal felt sticky with the sweat of high tension. Sweat beads also squeezed out of pores elsewhere on his body, adhered the clothing to his skin, formed irritating runnels along the bristles on his face.

He was sure he could smell the stink of his unwashed body, but then realised the smell of decay that had previously been strong in the brightly daylit room was now masked by the woman's perfume.

She went on: 'As you can see from this room, which is no better nor any worse, I think, than most of the others, the decor and furbishments leave something to be desired, Major. But all we really require are blankets for the poor souls to lay down upon and cover themselves with. I'm sure such people will not expect any degree of luxury when they are . . .'

Steele's breath felt like it was overheating where it was trapped between his lungs and gritted teeth behind his compressed lips. He was sure, as the woman's voice trailed away, he could hear his heart thumping. Then the hot breath almost burst noisily free of his body when he found his gaze fixed upon the bed. Where his duster lay across the rug.

The narrow bed had been stripped to the bare springs when

this woman last looked into the room. If she had ever looked in here? And remembered such details.

'Why, Major Tremlett, whatever is the matter?' she asked, sounded perplexed but also half afraid that she knew the answer to her question.

Steele felt his tension ease and opened his mouth wide enough so the stale air could trickle out soundlessly. This as he realised her concern had nothing to do with what she saw inside the room.

'You mentioned desire, Miss Marigold,' the man replied tautly. 'Desire is what is troubling me, woman. If you will permit me, I'd——'

She drew in her breath sharply.

He vented a soft moan.

Their footwear scraped on the bare floorboards of the landing.

'I certainly will not, sir!' she snapped, and her haughty tone sounded totally false now.

She lunge backwards, knocked the door open wider. It thudded against the palm of the hand Steele put up to keep it from hitting the gun he drew from his belt. The noise of the impact was masked by her small scream and the renting of ripped fabric.

She pulled up awkwardly, took a backward half step and got her feet tangled in the hem of her dress. Another scream sounded as she fell into Steele's line of sight, her arms flailing wildly as she struggled to regain her balance. Right then unconcerned that the bodice of her gown and an undergarment were ripped from neckline to waist, exposing the creamy mounds of her small, firm, brown-crested breasts.

'Miss Marigold, I never meant to——' the major started to excuse as he stepped into the room.

On his face, which Steele saw in profile, was a look of profound shock. But his voice became more husky as his desire was heightened by the sight of the woman's naked torso.

She hit the floorboards hard. Was too shocked to move, or perhaps she was stunned when her head cracked into the timber. Whichever, she remained with her arms flung wide to the sides, making no attempt to cover herself as the uniformed figure halted at her feet.

His expression altered to match his voice as he started to stoop over her, croaked: 'Miss Marigold, now it's done, you can't expect a man not to——'

She wrenched her head to the side, forcefully seeking not to look up at the towering form of the aroused man. And when she saw Steele the terror on her lovely face was instantly displaced by a plea for help. And she raised an arm, hand splayed in a tacit gesture that beseeched him to come to her aid.

Just as her lips began to move, to form the shape of a word she was not yet able to voice, Tremlett realised there was a third party in the room. He snapped his head round, sprayed tiny droplets of saliva as he vented an obscenity, dropped into a lower stoop as he fumbled to unfasten the buttoned flap of his hip holster.

The Navy Colt in the hand of the Virginian was already levelled at the uniformed man. Steele thumbed back the hammer, angled the revolver so its muzzle aimed at Tremlett's heart, squeezed the trigger. Saw the seemingly insignificant hole appear in the man's chest, left of centre, then a tiny amount of dark fluid that oozed out to stain his previously immaculate tunic. Before the man's hands fell limply to his sides and he went down hard on his knees. A look of desolation rather than one of pain contorted his distinguished features.

'If it helps any, feller,' Steele told him evenly, 'you died in action. Lieutenant Adam Steele, Army of the Mississippi. Was at Shiloh, anyway.'

Tremlett teetered on his knees, tried to say something, shook his head as if to signal to his killer he could not speak. Then he died, would have sprawled heavily across the legs of the woman had she not hurriedly dragged herself clear.

Then she rolled on to her hands and knees and scampered away into a far corner of the room. Where she used one hand to claw on the wall to drag herself upright while with the other she clutched at the torn dress bodice, pulled the mutilated fabric together.

'Lady, I'd like——' Steele started, broke off when he heard shouting voices far off beyond the front of the house.

The woman filled the silence within the room, masked out the distant sounds of voices but not the clatter of suddenly galloping hooves when she challenged vehemently, maybe

31

hysterically: 'You won't have the time before the major's men get here, Lieutenant!'

'Was about to say I'd like for you to put on my duster, cover yourself,' Steele told her and gestured with his free hand toward the bed as he thrust the revolver back under the belt at his belly.

'What?' She stared at the bed, had to shake her head to perhaps clear it of preconceived notions concerned with it as a bed, her state of undress and the way another man had tried to force himself upon her. Then what Steele had said was registered by her racing mind. And she blurted against the rapidly rising volume of sound from the approaching riders: 'Oh, I see! Oh, thank you! You mean . . . ! I guess I just didn't understand. I owe you so——'

'And I'm calling in the debt right away,' Steele interrupted her as she hurried to the bed.

She kept her back to him as she donned the long coat, fastened sufficient buttons to fully cover her upper body.

'Of course,' she agreed. And when she turned around he saw she had successfully suppressed for the moment her shock over what had taken place in this room. Now made a great effort to remain calm as she told him: 'Any woman would be immensely grateful to any man who saved her from what that ogre was about to do, sir! But I have to tell you, I cannot change my allegiance. You told the major you are a Rebel officer. The men approaching this house are loyal to Mr Lincoln and the United——'

'Lady, you know this house well,' he cut in on her. 'All I want is to get out of it. Without having to duck Yankee bullets. Show me the way I can do that and your debt's cleared. Whether your conscience will be doesn't bother me at all.'

There was a gravel driveway that led to the house from a pair of fallen-down wrought iron gates at the end of a rutted track. The leading horses galloped on to this, carrying the men close enough for their voices to be heard again, without the meaning of what they shouted reaching Steele and the woman. But obviously they were demanding to know the reason for the gunshot.

The woman seemed to be deaf to the sounds for stretched seconds, lost in consideration of what Steele said. Or maybe she was employing a delaying tactic while the Union soldiers rode closer: near enough now so the wheels of a wagon could be heard crunching on the gravel?

Steele was prepared to give her the benefit of the doubt for a moment longer. Then she nodded emphatically, said as she started across the room:

'Yes, that will be fine. If you escape from here unseen, the major's men will not be endangered in a gunfight. You will follow me?'

She paused beside the dead man a few feet from the threshold of the room, looked expectantly at Steele. Totally self-possessed again, her bearing aristocratic and her tone a match for the expression on her beautiful face when she told him: 'I give you my word you can trust me, sir.'

He shrugged, gestured she should go ahead of him through the doorway, said: 'Except for my life, all I've got to lose is what's left of my faith in human nature.'

She nodded in the manner of a woman used to having men do her bidding. Hurried out of the room and turned across the landing, to move along the hallway rather than going down the broad staircase.

Horses and a wagon were brought to a noisy halt on the turning circle of gravel at the foot of the porch steps. Men leapt heavily down.

'Major?'

'Miss Oaks?'

'Major Tremlett, we heard a shot!'

The voices of three anxious men. Steele could not tell if that was the sum total of Yankees out front of the house as he moved in the wake of the woman. Who did not look so elegant now, hurrying awkwardly in the restricting skirt of the dress and wearing the less than stylish duster.

Distance and the clatter of their feet on bare boarding acted to diminish the body of sound from outside. They reached the far end of the hallway as the big front door of the house was flung open. There was a moment of silence as Marigold Oaks and Adam Steele halted before what looked like the door to another bedroom. Then the metallic sounds of gun hammers being cocked was heard. Three, or more.

'Major Tremlett, sir! Are you in the house?'

The woman pressed a rigid forefinger to the centre of her

33

lips. With her other hand turned the knob and pulled the door open. Below, the same question as before was reiterated in a different form of words.

'Back stairs to the kitchen,' the woman whispered.

'After you,' Steele rasped.

She shook her head, scowled at him. 'I'll have to stay. Explain to them somehow. Please? Please hurry.'

Footfalls clattered on the flagstone floor of the entance hall. The men down there were whispering to each other now, their concern expanding to fear.

The look on the lovely face of the woman showed almost the same degree of pleading as she had directed up at him while she lay, her upper body exposed before the gaze of the Yankee major turned into a lusting animal. 'Trust me, I implore you,' she murmured. Then reached out a tentative hand, touched his upper arm. 'Please hurry.'

Footfalls ceased to clatter on the flagstones and rapped hollowly on the stairway. Steele held back a moment longer, then nodded curtly.

She withdrew her hand and he went by her. On to a tiny landing at the top of a narrow stairway with stone walls and wooden treads. A moment later she closed the door and pitch blackness surrounded him.

He started down cautiously, heard sounds from behind the door. Discerned her shriller tones among the voices of the men, but could not make out what anyone was saying. Had no inclinations to waste time finding out as he concentrated on descending the narrow stairway, on his guard against reckless haste: aware that if he stumbled the noise might give away his escape route to the Yankees.

Every breath he took, every creak of a stair, every brush of his shirt sleeve on the stone wall sounded inordinately loud. Then he was on a flat, square area of floor. Saw the line of light at the foot of a door to his right.

He felt for a knob, but snatched his hand away when he heard another door, in the room beyond this one, bang open. Then whispered voices.

He drew the Colt, snapped his head around to peer up the dark stairway as running footfalls sounded in the hallway, rising in volume.

His mind filled with a vivid image of Marigold Oaks' face as she urged him to trust her, recalled her shrill tone among the voices of the soldiers. And his lips parted to shape the same obscenity spoken by Major Tremlett just before he died.

He felt certain he was about to die, but unlike the Yankee officer, he was not about to go down alone. He would take at least one of the Bluebellies with him: a couple if he got that lucky. Or, if the fates were in a trading mood, he'd be happy for the whole bunch of men to survive if he could have the pleasure of blasting a killing bullet into the black heart of the beautiful woman.

He pushed his back against the wall: preparing to launch himself at the kitchen door. To burst it open. Surprise the men in the kitchen for the split second that could make the difference between killing one or killing more.

A soft click sounded behind him and the wall did not offer the support from which to start his lunge at the door. Then the door at the top of the stairway started to open. The one that gave on to the kitchen rattled. And the breath trapped inside Steele now was so hot it felt like it seared the membranes of his throat.

The Colt almost slipped out of his sweat-greasy hand.

He pressed himself backwards. Now heard a slight creak of hinges at the same time as an oath was snarled behind the door facing him.

'What's the Goddamn matter?'

'The lousy door's locked.'

'So the rapin' sonofabitch is trapped! Let's——'

Steele heard nothing more. For with a less obtrusive creak of hinges, the door through which he had unwittingly backed had closed of its own accord. And he stood in the same degree of pitch darkness as earlier. But this was a silent darkness, the silence drumming in his ears. An absolute silence, for nothing could be heard from the other side of the door.

Which was not a door in the conventional sense, he realised as he recalled the texture of the surface against his back while he readied himself to lunge at the kitchen door: rough, unplastered stone. Which he felt again on this side as he explored it with a hand. Failed to find timber, or a handle, even a crack to show there was a section of wall that could be opened

35

and closed like a door.

He was motionless for a moment, but then knew there was no need to hold his breath anymore. Next he felt confident enough of his safety on this side of the wall to strike a match. Closed his eyes against the dazzle of the flare, unconcerned others might see it. For if the place was soundproof, it followed light could not escape its confines.

He saw that he was at the head of another stairway, and he had been wise to strike the match. For three treads down the stairs took a sharp turn to the right unflanked by walls or bannisters, and descended into an expansive cellar.

Halfway down the stairs, where a fall to either side would not break any bones, he paused and looked more closely at his surroundings. A cellar with stone walls and a dirt floor. There was not the smell of damp he might have expected; instead, a faint smell of oil permeating the dominant aroma of mustiness.

This oily smell plainly emanated from the scores of cobweb-covered wooden crates that were stacked around three walls.

The match went out and Steele struck another to light his way to the foot of the stairway. He continued to clutch the Navy Colt in his other hand as he crossed to the wall opposite the stairs. Where there was a doorway hung with a pair of conventional wooden doors. Obviously it was through this entrance that the crates had been brought into the secret cellar.

They were secured with a heavy plank dropped into iron brackets at either side. It was simple enough to remove the piece of lumber. Then a hinge screeched in protest when Steele pulled open one of the doors. The only sound to follow this one was that of the Colt's hammer being cocked.

The fresh sweat that had broken out on his face was abruptly dried by a draught of cool morning air which wafted through the open doorway.

He struck a third match, and in the light of its flame that danced in the draught he saw the start of a six feet high and just as wide tunnel, the roof and walls shored up with stout timber, like in a mine.

His first impulsive instinct was to go through the doorway, hurry along the tunnel to discover where the fresh air was entering. But curiosity, allied with a powerful need to grasp any opportunity for revenge after the woman had betrayed him, caused him to hold back. Discover just what, smelling faintly of oil, was stored in the cobweb-draped crates.

It took him just a few minutes to do this. Then he wasted just a few seconds in reflecting on his good luck, and broke out into another sweat when he realised how it could have turned bad: recalled the way he had carelessly tossed aside burning matches.

Ten minutes later, all was ready. Maybe it had taken too long. But there was nothing he could do about that. He could only take the decision not to sacrifice more time to caution.

And so he struck one final match, dropped it deliberately, lunged out of the cellar and into the tunnel. Both hands, one of them clutching the revolver, thrust out in front of him.

He did not need to run blindly for more than a few moments, keeping his face toward the stream of cool air: that smelled even fresher against the acrid taint of burning behind him. For soon, daylight showed ahead. Just a little of it, here and there over a vertical area about ten feet square. But adequate to guide him to the end of the tunnel. Which turned out to be in the base of a rocky escarpment, the opening overgrown with thorny brush.

Steele scratched his right hand on the brambles as he used the knife from the boot sheath to hack a way clear of the tunnel entrance. He started to sweat freely again, despite the cool morning air that surrounded him now, because he could not be certain just when the contents of the crates stored in the secret cellar would explode: send a crushing blast along the hundred yards length of the tunnel.

An explosion powdered by God knew how much gunpowder. The blast driving before it countless rounds of small calibre shot and the twisted metal of thousands of disintegrated muskets and carbines.

Maybe!

Then he was clear: racing away from the escarpment, sucking at the blood from the cuts on his hands. Cursing himself for not having worn his buckskin gloves. Cursing at the stinging pain of the tears in his skin. More vehemently cursing the beautiful woman who had betrayed him.

Then, as rage and exertion had him struggling to breathe, he vented a stream of obscenities at the failure of the ancient arms store to explode.

This had always been a possibility. For the flintlock action weapons which required shot rather than cartridges, and vast quantity of gunpowder, had plainly been stored in the secret cellar for a very long time. The cache amassed by an eccentric man and his three spinster daughters to . . .

Supply a war foreseen long before the attack on Fort Sumter? Left undisturbed for at least ten years, if Marigold Oaks was to be believed. And at that time there had been no reason for her to lie to Tremlett. Which side were the arms intended for in the north-south conflict? Or maybe they had been intended for some other war? For the Texans against Mexico? Or a war not fought on US soil?

Or the War for Independence?

But what the hell did it matter? To Steele it mattered only that, despite the dust-dry atmosphere in the cellar, the gunpowder must have lost its explosive property. Maybe had not even been able to sustain the flame he had started as a fuse to——

There was a far off dull thud. Like the firing of a single piece of heavy ordnance many miles away. He slithered to an unsteady halt on ground still sodden from the rain last night, dropped his punished hand to his side as other, much louder sounds reached him: beat against his ears with the effect of a whole battery of artillery pounding at a target.

A vicious killer's grin spread across his youthful face as he started forward. With less frenetic haste than before, heading for the collapsed wrought iron gates where the rutted track ended and the gravel driveway of the house began.

When he reached the once impressive entrance to the formerly immaculate grounds of the now derelict house, the stench of burning filled his nostrils. And he dropped to the wet ground, and covered his head with his arms as chunks of masonry, roof slates, window glass and ironwork started to crash down among the trees inside and outside the crumbled boundary wall.

A few moments later he rose and peered along the driveway between the overgrown lawns, confirmed what he suspected when he heard Marigold Oakes and Tremlett discussing the purpose to which the house would be put: before the beauty of the woman had driven the major into a fit of uncontrollable lust.

Several Negroes, at least a dozen, were running in terror or were sprawled on the gravel near a covered US Army wagon. Some of them were bleeding, as were the four spooked horses in the traces of the wagon. Had been struck by debris, hurled far and wide, from what was now an immense pile of burning and smoking, blackened rubble.

So the house was to have been used as a stopover for escaping slaves; an extension of the underground railroad that had been operating for many years before the war between the states started, shipping them north and over the border into Canada.

One of the running men, forehead and an arm bleeding heavily from jagged wounds, saw the Virginian standing between the posts of the fallen gates. He altered course, staggered toward Steele, eyes wide with terror, mouth gaping to suck clean air into his lungs seared by the burning air of the massive blast.

'Massah, massah!' he blurted as he stumbled to a halt fifteen feet from Steele. 'You help us? You with Missy Oaks and the major and the other——'

'What happened to her and the soldiers, boy?' Steele broke in.

The Negro glanced back at the smouldering ruin beyond the far end of the drive, answered morosely: 'They is all gone, massah. All inside when the house went up like the Devil hisself had opened a hole into it from hell.'

When he returned his wide-eyed gaze to Steele he saw a ghastly grin of evil pleasure on the bristled face of the white man. Knew he could not expect help from this quarter. Worse, the man with the pistol under his belt looked like he was getting ready to finish off anyone who escaped death in the explosion.

But then, instead of drawing the Colt, Steele moved his right hand up to his mouth, sucked more blood that had oozed from the scratches, said as he turned away from the uncomprehending black man: 'Yeah, feller, war sure can be hell. Especially when there's a piece involved.'

2

The motley bunch of road agents worked fast and efficiently to rob the held-up stage and its passengers.

The fat and ugly Thelma Cowley was firmly in control of the others: had Daryl and Belle keep the passengers covered while she, Ricky and the dark-complexioned Mel opened up the contents of the front and rear boots of the Concord, and the luggage on the roof.

Belle demonstrated that she was no stranger to guns: for if the Colt Hartford revolver model rifle was new to her previously, she had worked out how to use it while she utilised it as a cane. For she kept it levelled steadily from her slender hip, thumbed back the hammer, curled a finger to the trigger and showed a grim smile of something akin to pleasurable intent to kill while she raked the rifle back and forth along the line of three men and one woman.

This, as the passengers, complying with her growled reminder, took off their jewellery and emptied their pockets of cash: tossed it all into a heap on the ground.

Nobody checked to see if anyone had held anything back. Nor were they searched for concealed weapons which, Steele thought, would only have brought to light the knife in the sheath strapped to his ankle.

Supreme confidence was doubtless the reason why they were not searched for weapons: and the scowling Daryl and smiling Belle certainly never relaxed their vigilance for a part second. While as for the jewellery and cash: that was nothing more than a welcome bonus. It was to be expected the passengers would have some of both, but it was not the prime reason for the hold-up. Likewise, the contents of value they found in the roof luggage and boots: some other items of jewellery, good quality men's and women's clothing and George Rutherford's sample case filled with carpentry tools which a joyful Mel confiscated.

It was the padlocked crate, stencilled with the name of a San Francisco bank, that was the major prize of the hold-up.

This was too heavy for Thelma Cowley to lift out of the rear boot and she had Mel and Ricky manhandle the crate off the stage. Then everyone ducked away from the ricochets as Ricky blasted three bullets into the padlock before it broke open. Tightly packed inside the crate were half a dozen gold bars which gleamed lustrously in the bright sunlight as the bullion was transferred from the box to a pair of saddlebags.

The rest of the loot was stowed in other saddlebags or wrapped in bedrolls. Then the rifle and two revolvers carried by Ezra and Steve were emptied of ammunition, which was confiscated, and the weapons were hurled to the side.

Belle swung up behind Daryl and her mother hauled herself into the saddle of Mel's horse so the man had to mount behind the heavily-built woman.

'It's been a pleasure doin' business with you folks,' Thelma announced as she, Daryl and Ricky took up their reins: less than fifteen minutes after the stage was forced to a halt. 'Just a lousy shame somebody had to try to be a hero, got him and his partner killed.'

Daryl obviously did not recognise the implicit threat, and snarled: 'Don't nobody try to follow us, okay?'

'They'd better not!' Belle augmented, and caused the scowl on his fleshy face to deepen as she hugged him tightly around the waist with one arm.

Her mother pointed out: 'You got the stage and a full team of healthy horses. Guess one of the men can drive it on into Bending, then be on your way with a new driver and shotgun from there. And just be grateful all you lost was a few trinkets and couple of bucks.'

Steele said: 'I'll be grateful if you'll leave that rifle of mine, ma'am.'

'Uh?'

'Your daughter has my rifle. I wouldn't expect you to leave the bullets in it.'

'Belle?' Mrs Cowley queried.

'It's got a fancy plate fixed to the stock, Ma,' the younger woman answered, a whine in her voice. 'Gold for sure. And I don't figure we got the time to get it off the rifle right here and now.'

Thelma Cowley glanced briefly at the rifle her daughter held up, exhibiting the plate engraved with an inscription that stated the weapon was presented to Steele's father by Abraham Lincoln. Then she said:

'Sorry, Mr Steele. But, like you seen, we got us a hankerin' for gold. Let's go, boys.'

She led the way, tapping her heels against the flanks of the doubly burdened horse to start him forward at an easy walk. Ricky, riding the horse laden with the gold bars was next. And then Daryl moved his animal along at the rear, Belle holding on to him more tightly than ever with one arm while with the other hand she kept the Colt Hartford sloped to her shoulder, thumb on the uncocked hammer, finger crooked around the trigger. Rode with her head turned to show a half grin-half grimace until the line of three horses carrying five riders went from sight over the crest of the hill where the men had first appeared to the stage driver and guard.

'My, I truly thought we were goners for sure after they killed the two men,' Rutherford muttered breathlessly, drew out a large handkerchief and mopped the sweat beaded on his brow. 'The other two times it happened to me, there was a lot of shooting, but no killing.'

Delores Townsend complained: 'Alvin, I don't feel very well.'

'I'm not feeling too hot myself, dear,' her husband answered.

Steele shifted his unblinking gaze from the top of the hill where the road agents had gone from sight. Saw at once that Townsend's face was chalk white and he looked about to keel over in a faint from the effects of delayed shock. His wife seemed only to be suffering a sense of angry loss as she glowered down at the dusty ground where the jewellery and money had been heaped.

The Virginian reached out to grasp an elbow of the pallid, suddenly swaying man. Kept him on his feet and steered him to the side of the stage, lowered him to sit on the steps below the open door.

'Thank you so much, I'm so sorry for being such a helpless fool,' Townsend forced out of his tight, dry throat.

'Just rest there awhile,' Steele told him, moved away from

the Concord toward the front of the six horse team.

Mrs Townsend uttered a low cry, immediately forgot what had been bothering her, struck by genuine concern for her sick husband as she went to stoop beside him.

Rutherford offered: 'I had a flask of good brandy in my carpetbag. If those killers didn't steal it.'

'I'd be most grateful for a sip, sir,' Townsend groaned miserably.

'But Alvin, you don't drink!' his wife told him as Rutherford began to rummage among the scattered luggage.

Townsend told the woman tautly: 'I think now is a good time to find out why it is people do, Delores.'

They were all too involved with what concerned them to notice what occupied Steele. Until he led a pair of horses to the rear of the Concord. Then, as Townsend choked on the fiery liquid and his wife thumped him on the back, Rutherford started to ask:

'What on earth is the reason for——'

'It's important I get back what was taken from me,' the Virginian broke in as he hitched one of the horses to the rear of the stage with a length of driving rein.

'But surely——'

'I'll need a mount,' Steele interrupted the perplexed drummer again. 'And whoever drives the stage to Bending will find it easier to handle with four horses instead of five of them in the traces.'

'But what do you hope to achieve by pursuing such a group of cold-blooded murderers?' the woman asked. 'You don't even have a gun.'

'That's right, ma'am, my rifle,' Steele told her.

'And the money and valuables that were stolen, you'll——' the hardware drummer started, broke off when his eyes met the level gaze of those above the thick beard.

'If I find anything that doesn't belong to me, I'll hand it over at Bending, feller,' Steele replied evenly. 'Or lodge it at the local sheriff's office if those it was stolen from aren't around.'

'Quite so,' Rutherford said lamely.

'Delores and I will be staying at the farm of our daughter and son-in-law, sir,' Alvin Townsend said, to fill a disconcerting silence.

Steele nodded, grasped the bridle of the chosen black gelding with one white foreleg and led him at a measured pace to the top of the hill, strongly conscious of the perhaps mistrustful eyes of the three stranded passengers as they fixed their gazes upon his back.

But he was more concerned at the possibility that the road agents had left behind somebody to ensure there was no immediate pursuit. And he breathed a silent sigh of relief when nobody yelled a warning or exploded a shot at him as he crested the rise and saw the terrain ahead was as heavily wooded as that through which they had been travelling all morning.

Steele surveyed the thickly timbered, spectacularly rugged country of the lower Sierra Nevada range spread to the south, and reflected that the supreme confidence of the Cowley women and the men they partnered would not allow them to consider they had failed in any aspect of the holdup. They would be sure to believe they had frightened the stage passengers into not giving chase. For as Delores Townsend had pointed out, what chance did an unarmed man—or even one with a knife—have against five people amply supplied with firearms?

But first the Virginian had a more immediate problem with which to contend. Horses used by stage line companies were just part broken in. They would submit to being put into traces with others of their own kind. Were even ready to haul a heavy rig for fifteen or twenty miles at a stretch over all kinds of terrain at whatever speed was demanded by the driver. Sure in their equine minds that at the end of each regular stint there would be feed, water and a snug place to bed down.

They were not schooled for, and did not take kindly to, being mounted. With or without a saddle between their backs and the rumps of riders.

But Adam Steele knew horses. Maybe he had not been able to ride one before he could walk: but the time between the two childhood attainments had not been so very long. And throughout his youth and young manhood he had lived among and spent much time astride the finest bloodstock animals when he hunted, or the meanest kind of quarterhorses while he worked on his father's plantation. In the war he had gotten to know cavalry horses, whatever kind of animals the CSA army

44

had been able to secure. And along all the trails he rode through until he came to the Providence River Valley he had experienced the most passive to the most ornery of animals.

He had never given up on one, and during the time he had been a horse breeder at Trail's End it had become more important than ever not to let an animal get the better of him. Which he had achieved by the same rules he applied now to this baleful-eyed gelding which was baring its teeth at him: showed him respect melded with the authority of a master's hand.

He spoke softly but firmly, applied force to the reins only when the circling animal sought to wrench free as he thought he was going to be mounted. At all other times, Steele matched his moves with his tone of voice, trying to coax the uneasy animal into a sense of security.

The horse remained mistrustful, but for long stretches of seconds he thought he was winning the battle of wills. Until, maybe ten minutes after the process had started, Steele combined force with speed of movement. Leapt astride the broad back of the big, strong animal. Clung to his mane with gloved fists, gripped his flanks with thighs, knees and booted feet. While the horse reared and bucked, whinnied and snorted, broke into a lathered sweat as he strove to unseat the unwanted burden from his back, gave vent to his rage when he could not.

It seemed to go on for an eternity, but Steele realised when the struggle began to subside and he was able to adjust to a reality outside of the spinning, tilting, twisting, fast changing light and shade of the violent episode, that it could not have been so very long.

The horse, already weary from the morning haul, could not sustain such a vigorous protest for longer than a couple of minutes. While Steele, battered and bruised, gasping for breath and sodden with sweat, knew he would not have been able to stay on the back of the enraged animal any longer than that.

Now, in the quiet aftermath of the wild struggle, he did not give in to the urge to relax, lower his body against the neck of the trembling gelding. For this might be the kind of horse with intelligence to take advantage of a man showing weakness. He had dealt with just such animals in the past. So he remained upright on the gelding's back as he stroked the sweat-lathered neck, spoke gibberish in a tone that was firm and soft like before. Consolidated his mastery of the beast while at the same time he congratulated him on being such a fine animal. Which he truly felt.

Then he asked for a walk: used the reins rather than his heels, which this gelding was not schooled to understand. The horse responded with a final aggrieved snort, which was fine with Steele, who had little time for animals without spirit. Those which were broken in every sense of the word: usually by men who had no feel for horseflesh.

'Mr Steele, are you all right?' Alvin Townsend called from beyond the rise.

The Virginian put his new-found rapport with the animal to another test: asked for a turn, back to the crest of the high ground. Reined him in when he saw the still ashen-faced, business-suited man hurrying up the hill from the Concord, where the man's wife and the drummer were gathering up the bags and suitcases and their discarded contents which had been strewn around by the road agents.

The corpses were no longer in sight.

'Oh!' Townsend gasped, pulled up in surprise as the mounted Virginian showed on the brow of the hill. 'What with all the noise, I feared you had come to some harm from the horse.'

'Nice of you to be concerned,' Steele told him. 'The horse and me had a few troubles adjusting to each other, feller. But like you can see, I've gotten on top of the problem.'

Townsend blinked, nodded, swallowed hard. And got some of the colour back in his cheeks when Steele asked:

'You people about ready to be on your way?'

The previously grey-faced man was now suddenly flushed as he glanced back toward the Concord, quickly returned his attention to Steele, blurted: 'Yes! Yes indeed. I'm afraid I had to withdraw while they took care of the corpses. Covered them and placed them inside the stage. I'm ashamed to say . . . Well, I can't help being the way I am, I suppose. Delores—my wife—has always been much better at such things than me. We'll all ride on top of the stage, of course.'

'Fine. I'm glad that between you, you managed to——'

'Mr Steele!' Townsend blurted as the Virginian was about to tug on the reins, wheel his mount.

'Feller?'

'I'm a useless individual in these kind of troublesome situations. Always have been. I'm just not a practical man. Nor do I have the stomach for anything——'

'You already said you can't help being the way you are,' Steele said.

Townsend shook his head, said a little irritably: 'Please let me finish, sir. I'm not a wealthy man by any means, but my wife and I are comfortably provided for.'

He turned to look down at the Concord again, and Steele prompted:

'You want to get to the point, Mr Townsend? I'm in kind of a hurry to leave.'

The man swallowed hard again, nodded vigorously, said in a rush: 'Yes, yes, of course. Every moment wasted allows the culprits to get even further away. It's that ... well, my wife's jewellery means a great deal to her. If you should recover it, I'm willing to reward you for your trouble, sir.'

He could not hold the Virginian's level gaze as Steele started to explain:

'Mr Townsend, I'm going to——'

'In the sum of one thousand dollars, Mr Steele!' Townsend blurted, clearly worried he would not get said what he wanted to say unless he forced it out in a hurry. 'I'm a useless, empty individual. It seems to me the least I can do is ... What do you say, sir?'

'If all goes well, I'll see you in Bending, Mr Townsend,' Steele answered, tugged on the reins to turn the horse now.

'Quite so. And you'll have Delores's jewellery, if all goes well?'

'Money talks, feller,' Steele drawled, touched the brim of his hat. 'But actions speak louder than words, uh?'

The Fugitives

During that period of his life covered in the contemporary stories of the second two STEELE'S WAR books, the Virginian seemed to be a married man while he ran a small town grocery store. The incident which follows took place between the end of *The Storekeeper* and the start of *The Stranger*.

On slow business days Adam Steele often allowed his mind to wander. It helped to while away the time. On this hot and dusty day, business was at its slowest as he stacked shelves and wondered yet again what he had gotten himself into.

A born and raised Virginian who once thought he could never be truly happy until he attained something close to the birthright he lost because of the War Between the States, what was he doing here in this store in this Texas town?

Waiting for good things to happen, he guessed!

The grocery store on the main street of White Rock, a stage stop community on the trail between Abilene to the north and San Antonio to the south, was a small one. But a lot of people claimed White Rock had potential for growth, and as the town spread in area and grew in population, it was surely possible the store would expand.

And Adam and Lucy Steele, now scraping a bare living by keeping the grocery open from dawn to dusk seven days a week could get rich. Not as rich as Steele would have been if the destiny of the United States of America had not robbed him of his inheritance, of course. Hell, he'd need to own a string of stores with branches on the smartest streets of New York, Chicago and San Francisco to achieve that. But the vagaries of life forced a man to make compromises. And with a larger store in a booming town, he could amass sufficient wealth to give his new wife some of the luxuries sadly lacking at present.

Not that she wasn't already much better off than she would have been had he not rescued her from the man she had come west to marry. For she would have wound up a ...

He growled a word of censure at himself and speeded up the chore of stacking new stock on the shelves behind the counter at the rear of the store. Cans and jars and packages that had been delivered from his Abilene supplier yesterday afternoon.

Perhaps it was because he regarded this as one of the least enjoyable storekeeping tasks that he found his mind drifting into the area of dark memories. Usually he endeavoured to steer his train of thought to the bright future he hoped to share with his green-eyed, redheaded new wife, five feet three inches tall, slimly built, and just thirty years old.

They had both had their tough times in the past, although she had not told him much about herself: just as he had held back much of what had happened to him before they met at the Gold Gulch way station over in Arizona Territory. Had themselves, it was accurate to say, a whirlwind romance: which led to an impulsive marriage at an Apache *rancheria*.

Found their way by chance to White Rock and this store which had been for sale. There were a few other stores on the street, along with a saloon, a bank, a stage depot and telegraph office, a church, a meeting hall and some houses. These comprising a town to supply the wants and needs of the farming and ranching families on the places scattered far and wide over the surrounding country.

It was weatherbeaten country and White Rock was a weatherbeaten town: defencelessly exposed to the blue northers that roared across the Texan plains, did not blow themselves out until they crossed the Rio Grande into Mexico.

But for some inexplicable reason it had looked good to Adam and Lucy Steele when they rode into town, and they bought George Dalton's grocery store on mortgage with no more thought than they had given to getting married. Found themselves quickly accepted as the new store owners by small town folks who could spot square pegs in round holes, were genuinely pleased this high born Virginian and his Mississippi belle of a wife had been able to adapt.

Then a bank robbery compelled Steele to bring out from the

closet his Colt Hartford rifle, the knife in the boot sheath and the kerchief that was actually an Oriental weapon of strangulation. To ride with a posse composed of small town merchants and businessmen, headed up by the part time sheriff of White Rock.

What happened when the posse cornered the bank robbers had dramatically demonstrated just what kind of man Steele had been before he came to this town and purchased the store. But the initial repugnance at his cold-blooded violence had soon been transcended by gratitude. In those circumstances they had needed a man like Steele, even if they felt unable to approve of his methods.

All was fine again now. Of those people who used the store—almost every household in the town and surrounding area—few treated Steele as anything other than the owner of a country town grocery.

The few who did not were women, married and single, and spanning a wide age range. Who were inclined to direct surreptitious glances at him—and some even made comments—which revealed that they were intrigued by him: were more interested in him than respectable ladies should be in a married man who had obviously had a more exciting past than the average small town storekeeper.

But he had never given any encouragement to such women and . . .

When the bell above the door jangled this uncomfortably hot morning, Steele rose from where he had been crouched behind the counter. Saw on the threshold of the store a woman who was at the lower end of the age scale: just beyond the limit when she would have been a girl. A stranger in this isolated community which usually was visited only briefly by travellers riding the San Antonio to Abilene stage.

A brown-haired, brown-eyed, pale-faced woman in her mid-twenties, with a petite build and delicately pretty features. She wore a once smart blue dress which now was stained and dirtied by travel. And she carried a battered, wide-brimmed straw hat that was a match for the state of the dress. Her expression as she peered at Steele across the aromatic store suggested she felt as worn and limp as her outfit.

'Sir?' she queried softly.

50

'Help you, young lady?' Steele asked as he tightened the ties of his waist apron.

'I wonder, might I sit down for a while? The journey . . . and the heat of the day . . .'

There was a hard-seated, straight-backed chair just inside the doorway and she sank gratefully on to it before Steele could respond to her request. She tried to smile but failed. Perhaps mistook the Virginian's expression of concern for one of censure, for she hurried to excuse: 'I'll buy something if it's expected? A cool glass of sarsaparilla will be most welcome if you stock . . .'

Steele moved around the end of the counter. And perhaps she again misinterpreted his motives, for she made to rise from the chair. But she couldn't make it, fainted on her feet and corkscrewed awkwardly to the floor. Banged her knees, then a hip. Would have crashed her head against the floorboards had Steele not gotten to her side, stooped and caught her by the shoulders.

'Lucy!' he yelled, and looked around for something to serve as a pillow.

He saw a nearby open sack of dried peas, spilled a considerable amount of the contents as he dragged it into position beneath her head. He stayed crouched beside the senseless but evenly breathing woman as Lucy pushed through the bead-curtained archway that connected the store with the living quarters out back, a stairway to the bedroom above.

'Adam, you sounded——'

'I need a glass of water for a young lady who's fainted.'

'One of those who think you're such a mystery man?' she asked good naturedly. But, as always when the subject of her husband's female admirers was raised, Lucy's temper came to the simmer just beneath the surface.

'Nobody we know.'

Lucy was concerned now, as she urged: 'Well, don't leave her lying there, honey. Bring her into the parlour. I'll clear the couch ready.'

As his wife withdrew through the arch, Steele rose and stepped out through the doorway that was still open from when the woman entered the store.

The searing heat that was certainly partly to blame for the

51

young woman's faint seemed to possess a physical force as it hit his face. This area of Texas frequently suffered extremes of temperature, but it was the hottest day for years, early customers had said.

Because of the heat the street was empty of life, except for a swarm of lazily droning flies giving their irritating attention to a doleful-looking piebald pony immediately out front of the store. The animal was not hitched to the rail at the sidewalk, but he did not look like he wanted to wander off.

There was nobody to bring the town doctor in the event that the woman's faint signalled something more than heatstroke.

Lucy called: 'All right, Adam, I've got the couch ready for her!'

Steele turned back into the store as he made an indifferent double-take toward a distant movement in the shimmering heat haze to the south.

He picked up the limp and lightweight form, took care not to bang her head or feet against displays in the cramped store as he carried her across it, eased cautiously through the archway behind the counter.

The small parlour was furnished to the taste of the previous owner: an elderly widower with no wish to renew anything if it was still possible to patch it up. But it served the needs of the newcomers until they could afford better.

The couch on which Lucy had arranged cushions for a pillow was the most comfortable item of furniture in the room and, almost as if she relished its soft luxury, the unconscious woman sighed after Steele lowered her on to it.

'She asked for some sasparilla just before——' Steele started.

'A glass of plain water will be of greater benefit to her, Adam,' Lucy interrupted, went to the doorway that led to the kitchen. Then paused to ask as Steele rose from his crouch and turned away: 'Where are you going?'

'Her horse, out front. He looks to be in worse shape than she is.'

Despite how he made himself be polite toward even the most awkward of their customers—and the White Rock Grocery had its fair share of complainers—Lucy had discovered during their short marriage that her husband thought more highly of dumb animals than his fellow humankind. So she merely shrugged, continued on into the kitchen, but called after him:

'All right, Adam. But don't you think you can shirk your responsibilities in here. Remember, it was you brought in this waif and stray!'

Out on the deserted street Steele saw the moving figure to the south was larger than before in perspective: now was recognisable as a lone rider heading up the trail from San Antone.

He took hold of the weary gelding's bridle and the horse responded lethargically to being led along the shaded alley between the store and a house next door.

Out back of the grocery was a stable where he took longer than necessary attending to the needs of the horse. Then he ignored the store's back door that offered the quickest way to return to where Lucy was tending to the woman. Instead he ambled back along the alley, emerged on to the brilliantly sunlit street just as the clock in the bank a few doors away began to chime the hour of twelve.

He tried to tell himself he was taking his time because he wanted no part in reviving the woman: that was woman's work! But he admitted to himself with a sense of mild disgust that in truth he was impatient to see who was riding into town on the south trail. Which gave him a twinge of conscience as he recalled the line along which his thoughts had been wandering before the woman stepped into the store and collapsed.

He was keenly interested to see who was heading for town: which went totally against the grain of the kind of man he was before he and Lucy settled at White Rock. But it was natural for a citizen of a small backwater town to show interest in any break with routine. Hell, half the town would likely spill on to the street, the other half peer out, as soon as people realised a newcomer was approaching. So he ought not to feel disgusted at himself for harbouring such a natural interest in an unusual event: now he was the kind of man he had become!

The rider was close enough to be seen as a man. And it was only then Steele glanced at the sign on the dusty street with no name that ran through White Rock: less a street than just a building-flanked wider stretch of the trail. Saw without need of much study on such a hot, slow day that the woman had ridden her exhausted piebald into town from the same direction.

It was because the day was so blistering hot, he reasoned, that his grocery was not crowded with the more forthright of his fellow citizens, come to satisfy their curiosity about the first stranger to arrive in White Rock this morning.

Or was he kidding himself? Was he so ill-suited to small town life that he alone had an interest in passing-through strangers?

'Adam, Miss Stephenson is awake and wishes to thank you for your help,' Lucy said, her tone suggesting she would be put out if her husband did not come inside, accept his responsibilities as she had requested earlier.

Steele stooped to pick up the straw hat the woman had dropped when she collapsed. Then he closed one of the pair of double doors she had opened. Which on a breezeless day such as this helped a little to keep out the heat. On days when the air was stirring, closing the doors kept out some of the fine Texas dust.

'Somebody else is heading up the trail from the south,' Steele reported as he crossed to where Lucy waited, holding the strands of beads aside.

'What was that?' the woman called from the parlour as Steele noticed his wife had changed out of her drab and shapeless housework dress into one that was white and crisp and clean. She had also washed grimy sweat off her face and tidied her copper-coloured hair.

Lucy pulled a face at her husband, like she was trying to signal something to him. But when he shrugged his failure to understand, she acknowledged it with a shrug of her own. And a slight change of expression signified she knew there was no time for explanations right then. She opened the bead curtain wider, ushered him ahead of her.

In the parlour he saw Miss Stephenson was sitting up on the couch now. Her face was not so pale and she clutched a half full glass of water in both hands on her lap. The expression on her pretty face, now with a patch of pink at the centre of each cheek, showed much the same degree of apprehension that had sounded in her voice. Along with a trace of faint hope, maybe.

'You dropped this, ma'am,' Steele told her, put the hat on a nearby table.

'Yes, thank you,' she acknowledged quickly. 'You said somebody was coming toward this town from the south?'

'Right.'

'A man, I expect?'

'Looks like, but it's hard to tell over the distance, Miss Stephenson.'

'Call me Ruth, please. Oh, so you can't tell if he's young or older?'

'No.'

'Ruth is from a town called Grover, down near the Mexican border,' Lucy explained. 'She hoped to meet a friend in White Rock.'

'Anyone we know?'

'No!' Ruth blurted and stood up. But she had forgotten about the glass she held and it spilled water down her dress. 'Oh, I'm sorry!'

'No harm done,' Lucy assured her, went to the woman and took the glass. 'Water won't hurt anything.'

'Thank you, you're very kind, Mrs Steele. Mr Steele, I was telling your wife, I'm meeting a young man here. My fiancé. But he's not from around here. His name is Frank Buchan and he lives near Lorenston. You haven't heard that he got here ahead of me?'

She was eager to hear his answer, but was also straining to pick up the first clop of a hoof on hard-packed ground outside.

'No,' Steele told her. 'And if he had, I reckon we would've known about it. White Rock being such a small town where not many strangers come by.'

She seemed more anxious by the moment, her head held in a listening attitude.

Lucy asked: 'Why didn't you meet your young man in Lorenston, Ruth? You had to come through there to get here.'

Lorenston was the next stage stop south of White Rock, fifteen miles away. Nothing more than the way station, a saloon and a scattering of mining camps where grubbers scratched bare livings, Steele recalled hearing.

'It's not a good place for a woman alone to have to wait for any length of time, Mrs Steele,' Ruth explained. 'That's what Frank wrote me. And when I rode through it in the middle of last night, I could see what he meant. It's not a nice looking town, like this one.'

She shuddered.

'You've been riding all night?' Lucy asked.

Ruth nodded. 'Most of it. What with not having so much sleep, and the heat of the day, I guess it's why I threw the faint the way I did. I truly am sorry for the trouble I caused. I felt ill and your store was the first place I saw where I figured I might get some shade before——'

'There's no need for you to apologise for anything at all, Ruth,' Lucy assured her. 'But your fiancé has something to answer for, allowing you to——'

'Oh, I don't mind what discomforts I have to endure so long as I can be with Frank,' Ruth broke in resolutely.

'Well, I certainly hope it is Mr Buchan who's almost here!' Lucy countered, a little tautly. 'And he has something planned. White Rock doesn't have facilities for strangers to stay. There's just a small waiting room at the stage line depot.'

'I'll go there, if it isn't Frank——'

'I'm sure they won't object to you waiting there,' Lucy cut in. 'But it's only for passengers while the horses are being changed. And they don't have rooms for overnight guests.'

'That's all right, Mrs Steele, Mr Steele,' she assured hurriedly and went to get her hat as her nervous gaze switched constantly between the husband and wife.

Lucy looked pointedly at Steele, and was now able to explain the meaning of what she had tried to convey with an earlier expression. 'Ruth said she was prepared to pay to stay here, but I explained we have just the one bedroom, honey.'

Before Steele could respond, Ruth went on insistently:

'It really is perfectly all right. You have both done enough for me already. If I have to sleep rough, it won't be the first time since I left Grover. With luck, though, that'll be Frank coming up the trail now. And he'll know what to do. Probably we'll be on our way to Abilene right off.'

'I think you should delay leaving until after the heat of the day has cooled some, Ruth,' Lucy told her. 'The sun can do great harm to a person. And especially after you've already——'

Ruth held back at the archway, gave the Steeles a shy smile as she said: 'I appreciate the advice as much as everything else you have done for me. But it'll be Frank who'll tell me what's right from now on.'

56

Then she turned, went out into the store. Steele held aside the bead curtain as Lucy came to stand beside him, the woman hurried out from behind the counter and crossed to the double doorway. She paused there for a moment, to take in a deep breath before she jammed on her hat, pulled open one of the doors and stepped outside, blurted:

'My horse!' She lunged to the front of the sidewalk, peered to the left and right. 'It's gone!'

Steele went toward her, but before he was halfway across the store, could begin to tell her the piebald was in the stable, Ruth Stephenson vented a throaty laugh, clapped her hands like an excited child. And gazed fixedly southward, said in a husky whisper:

'Oh, Frank, thank God it's you!'

Then she showed Steele a smile of joyful pleasure and explained: 'It's him, it's Frank. It's all going to be all right now!'

'I'm pleased for you,' Steele said as he stepped outside and looked toward the rider. Saw him now as a tall, leanly-built, black-clad figure astride a grey horse. Steele was not able to determine yet whether the rider was young or old, but clearly she could recognise her fiancé. He told her: 'Your horse hasn't been stolen or run off. I put him in our stable. Which is where he ought to be left, to rest up for awhile, before you head for Abilene.'

'Frank'll know what to do,' she answered absently.

'Even if you can make it many miles in this heat, your horse won't,' Steele added.

'Oh, I'm sure Frank will know exactly what we are to do!' she insisted, more forcefully, and stepped down off the sidewalk. But immediately she returned to the shade of the awning when she felt the pull power of the noontime sun blazing down upon her.

'See what I mean?' Steele added evenly.

He swept his gaze along the street in both directions and felt a mild sense of satisfaction that his earlier prediction had been proved partially correct. Maybe half the town's population had not spilled out on to the sun-seared street since the clop of slow-moving hooves could he heard, but several doors were cracked open and a lot of curtains twitched as his fellow citizens checked on the newcomer.

'Oh, I feel so ... so totally exhausted!' Ruth gasped.

This time Steele was close enough to reach out, put his arms around her to keep her from falling as she almost fainted again.

'Hey, you let her be!' the black-clad man yelled, thudded in his heels to command a gallop from the point where the open trail became the street. And dropped a hand to his side, jerked it up, pointed his arm forward, sunlight glinting on the dull metal of the revolver he had drawn.

'Adam!' Lucy shrieked out of the doorway immediately behind Steele and Ruth.

'Frank, no!' Ruth muttered from the brink of unconsciousness as she inwardly fought the need to give in to the demands of her punished body and struggled physically to break free of Steele's hold on her.

There seemed in Buchan's attitude astride the galloping horse a brand of uncontrollable rage. But at the final moment before he squeezed the revolver's trigger, as Steele knocked aside his wife and jerked Ruth through the doorway into cover, he saw something about the scene at the doorway of the White Rock Grocery that caused him to think again: in time to jerk his arm up. And the bullet cracked high. High enough so there was no sound of it impacting with the store's upper storey.

In the wake of the shot, Lucy yelled as she was sent sprawling to the floor. Then she snarled something that Steele was certain was an obscenity, as he was nearly shoved to the floor by Ruth as she fought to break free of his grip.

The galloping horse was reined to a rearing, snorting halt. The dust from beneath the lashing hooves drifted in through the store doorway and enraged Lucy still more as she struggled to her feet, coughing violently.

Steele submitted to Ruth's struggling demands to be turned loose, and glimpsed the fury on her face just before it was replaced by a kind of desolation. This in turn changed to the same degree of joy that had gleamed in her eyes when she first looked along the trail and recognised her fiancé.

She ran outside again then. She was still surely susceptible to the blistering strength of the sun, but was able to overcome its effects with the belief that everything really would be all right now Frank Buchan was here.

'Adam, just what the hell are we letting this couple get away with?' Lucy demanded through gritted teeth.

He knew his wife had the kind of temper that by tradition was supposed to come with the colour of her hair: and he saw she was in the grip of a reckless anger that could drive her into doing something she would surely regret when her emotions were under control again. He reached out with both hands and grasped Lucy by the shoulders, told her coldly: 'Stay here.'

'What?'

'You said this was my responsibility, woman!' he snapped. 'I'm going to handle it. Just stay here!'

They looked hard at each other, her green eyes glinting with high passion, his coal black ones emanating an icy light. And after stretched seconds of this, Lucy gave an almost imperceptible nod of her head: sufficient for him to know she meant it. She would do what he told her.

His nod was much more emphatic, then he released her, spun on his heels and strode out of the store, across the sidewalk and down on to the street. He blinked rapidly in the bright sunlight, saw the gunshot had drawn many more of his fellow citizens to where they could watch the scene on the street: which was comprised right then of a travel-wearied horse standing dolefully alongside a young couple locked in an embrace, their lips glued together.

The horse was between Steele and the couple until he cracked an open hand slap on its rump. And the grey spurted forward with a snort of complaint. The kissing couple sprang apart, the woman almost tumbling to the ground with the force of the shove from Buchan.

He was the first to see Steele, and the sight stirred panic in him. He once more went for his gun, clawed it out of the holster as he started to warn: 'Mister, you'd better not——'

He was a blue-eyed, blond-haired man of about the same age as Ruth Stephenson. Probably his evenly tanned face was handsome when he did not look so angry and so afraid. Now he looked almost ugly as Steele thrust his left arm forward, hand curled to fist around the barrel of the revolver. He wrenched it to the side and down, a move that caught Buchan off guard.

The younger man's sole aim for a stretched second was to retain his grip on the weapon as his body was forced sideways and downwards in the wake of the gun. And he failed to be

59

aware of Steele's right hand until, clenched into a fist as tight as that grasping the gun barrel, it cracked into the side of his jaw: sent him sprawling to the ground, still gripping the gun butt.

When Buchan was down on the street, Steele needed to bend low over him to retain his hold on the revolver. By choice he stooped even lower, so his voice could be heard above the shrieking of Ruth Stephenson as he told her fiancé:

'Let go of the gun, feller. Or I'll kick you where your wife-to-be wouldn't like it.'

'I figured you was——'

'Frank, he helped me!' Ruth shrieked to break in on his blurted explanation. 'Mr Steele and his wife! Don't do anything to——'

Frank released the gun, rolled over on to his back, and brought up a hand to drag across his mouth, wipe away the trickle of blood that had spilled from a cut lip.

Steele straightened up, stuck out his bottom lip and directed a stream of cooling air over his sweat-run face. He backed away from the scowling Buchan as Ruth bent over him, dabbed at the runnel of blood with a lacy handkerchief.

She spoke fast and low to him as he tried to avoid her ministrations while he struggled into a sitting attitude. But he was disorientated from being hit, exhausted from a long ride. She was strengthened by her love for him, concern about him.

Steele, feeling drained from the heat, the exertion and the expending of anger, backed up to the sidewalk, gained the shade of the roof. He still held the revolver, which he saw was a well worn Frontier Colt, the base of the butt scarred from being used as a hammer.

'Goodness, Adam, he might have killed you,' Lucy rasped as she came alongside him and gripped his arm, the concern on her face as strong as that expressed by the younger woman, helping Buchan to his feet.

'There are hotheads and there are killers, honey,' Steele said. 'And mostly hotheads don't kill.' Then he added lamely. 'And sometimes I get lucky.'

'Hey, you!' somebody called from within the saloon diagonally across the street from the grocery. 'Stranger! Is your name Buchan?'

It was Bart Dillon, the heavily-built, fifty-five-year-old

saloonkeeper who was also White Rock's part-time sheriff. He wore his leather apron with the money pouch at the front, but he was in process of pinning a five pointed tin star to his shirt front as he emerged from his premises, to show clearly that he had reverted from businessman to lawman. As the batwing doors swung noisily shut behind him, he demanded: 'You hear me, stranger?'

Buchan broke free of his fiancée and with a scowl of hot anger on his immaturely handsome face, was about to advance on Steele. But then he swung round at the sound of the other man's commanding tones, snarled: 'What if it is, mister?'

'Sheriff, when I'm wearin' this, son,' Dillon corrected flatly, stabbed a hooked thumb at the badge now firmly pinned to his chest. 'That answer mean you are Buchan? Frank Buchan?'

'Yeah! Yeah, that's who I am!'

Morning trade at the saloon had not been so good as the bulky pouch of Dillon's apron made it seem. For it was not money in the pouch. Instead, another Colt: which Dillon drew out and levelled at the young man, said as he thumbed back the hammer: 'You're under arrest, Mr Buchan. Advise you to come quiet, not give me any trouble.'

'No!' Ruth exclaimed.

'What the hell?' Buchan snarled, more enraged than ever after experiencing moments of shock. Then he wrenched his head up and from side to side, his eyes cracked almost closed against the brightness of the sky. But he was not seeking inspiration from the heavens: instead traced the line of the telegraph wire from the roof of the office to where it was strung between poles southwards into the heat shimmer. He looked back at the man with the gun advancing on him, and seemed suddenly as drained as his fiancée when she first arrived in White Rock. 'You heard from Sheriff Dwight Stephenson, I bet?'

'No!' Ruth said again, but there was no power in her voice this time.

White Rock did not have a regular jail-house, but a one-time storeroom in the rear of the small saloon had been converted for use as a cell when one was needed. It had wooden walls, but there were bars on the outside of the glazed windows. That was where Bart Dillon headed with Frank Buchan to lock him up, all the time having to contend with a barrage of protests of innocence from the young man. And his fiancée, who trailed them off the street and into the saloon. Their voices could still be heard for a long time after they went from sight.

By then, most of the townspeople had withdrawn from their vantage points and Steele sensed only scant and indifferent interest directed toward him as he moved away from the front of the store, to go get the grey gelding he had spooked into a bolt along the street.

The animal seemed to recognise the man who had abused him, eyed the Virginian resentfully. But he was too weary to get involved in a battle of wills and submitted without protest to being led by the bridle back along the street, down the alley and into the stable already crowded with three horses. But the shade, feed and water were better than any combination of creature comforts that awaited outside and the gelding remained placid while Steele unsaddled him.

'Yeah, I know,' Steele said as he sensed somebody at the doorway of the stable. 'It's none of my concern and I should let Bart Dillon have Grant Erland take care of the animal down at the livery.'

A man Steele had mistaken for Lucy growled huskily: 'I don't give a damn who takes care of the horse, mister. Just give me them there saddlebags and you can do whatever the hell you like.'

Steele turned just his head to look at the man who was of middle years, medium height and build, with an unshaven face adorned by a straggly grey moustache. He was dressed in a similar manner to Frank Buchan, except he wore an old suit jacket over his dark-hued Western trail-riding outfit, all the clothing sweat- and dirt-stained from long travel. He, too, wore a gunbelt with the holster tied down to his right thigh.

Steele could not see much of the revolver in the holster because the man's right hand was draped over the butt, tightened into a fist as the Virginian swung around to face him.

'The owner of this stuff may be in jail, but he still has rights, feller,' Steele said evenly. 'His property still belongs to him.'

'Don't try to teach me anythin' about prisoners' rights, mister,' the man at the doorway answered, his face and voice expressing impatient, soured anger. 'The name's Dwight

Stephenson, sheriff of Grover. Where nobody breaks the law and gets away with it.'

'Sheriff of this town is Bart Dillon and he's the law——'
Steele started to respond to Stephenson, whose name was not a coincidence. He had heard Ruth yelling something about her lawman father as she trailed Dillon and Buchan into the saloon. The Virginian broke off what he was saying when the Grover sheriff suddenly drew his revolver. Another Frontier Colt that probably had not been used as a hammer very often.

'I know who the local sheriff is, mister! I sent him a wire askin' him to arrest Frank Buchan. So, like I said, don't try to teach me the law. I know my badge doesn't mean anythin' in his jurisdiction. But I got the right to look for evidence of a crime anyplace. And evidence is what you're holdin', mister. So hand over them bags.'

'Don't do it, Mr Steele, please!' Ruth Stephenson pleaded from the yard between the rear of the store and the stable.

Her father sent a fast glance toward her. And Steele glimpsed his wife alongside the distraught-sounding woman as the lawman returned his attention to the stable interior, thrust the Colt forward a few inches to emphasise its threat.

'You don't want to involve yourself in this business which is none of yours, mister,' Stephenson said, tone as threatening as his stance.

'Trouble is, I already did,' Steele answered as the two women halted a few feet behind Stephenson.

Lucy started to implore: 'But you don't have to be any longer, Adam. Not now——'

'Father, what are you trying to do?' Ruth broke in.

'Keep you from throwin' yourself away on a no good thief!' he hurled at her.

'He isn't that!' she yelled. 'He isn't anything of the kind, I know it!'

'Steele, that your name?' Stephenson asked.

'Right.'

'If you won't hand over the saddlebags, will you open them up?' He looked down at the gun in his hand, grunted like he detested the thing, then thrust it back in the holster. 'Prove to this lovestruck daughter of mine——'

'No!' Ruth snarled, lunged forward and snatched the gun

out of her father's holster. She backed off, clutched the Colt in both hands, pulled back the hammer with both thumbs as she aimed it at arm's length.

'Ruth, what are you doin', girl?' Stephenson asked her in deep shock as he turned, pressed his back against a side of the doorframe.

'You can't——' Lucy croaked, and caught her breath, took several backward steps.

Steele got to the doorway in time to see the younger woman swing the gun, draw a bead on his wife.

'I'm doing it, Mrs Steele,' Ruth said, suddenly sounding icily calm, in total control of herself. 'And I'll shoot you, along with anyone else I have to if you people don't do what I ask.'

'Easy, girl,' her father urged, made to step away from the threshold of the stable.

'You take it easy, feller!' Steele snarled, as Ruth's hands tightened their grip around the butt of the gun and she uttered a low, almost animal-like growl. 'It's my wife's life on the line.'

'Ruth won't do anythin' so stupid as to——'

'I'll do whatever I have to do to keep Frank!' Ruth broke in.

'Don't even think for one second she won't!' Lucy said, slowly and distinctly, gazing fixedly at the once more ashen-faced woman aiming the gun at her.

Steele did a double-take at his wife, to see how hard she needed to work at seeming so calm and unafraid for her life. It cost her no visible effort.

'I appreciate it, Mrs Steele,' Ruth said. 'And now I'll thank you, Mr Steele, if you'll resaddle our horses. We're going to leave. And it'll be much better if nobody gets hurt because of what we want to do.'

Steele did not hesitate before he turned and went back into the stable, wondering if anyone realised he still had Buchan's gun stuck in his belt: until now concealed behind the saddlebags he had taken off the young fugitive's horse.

While he did as Ruth had asked, neither hurrying nor taking unnecessary time with the saddling chores, Steele heard her say something that did not carry into the stable. But her father was still at the doorway and his answer was clearly audible inside.

'The letter he wrote you didn't burn all away, Ruth. When I woke up and found your note, I saw the ashes and the unburnt paper in the hearth. So I knew you were goin' to meet him here and I wired the local sheriff to arrest Buchan soon as he showed up in town.'

His daughter, her throat constricted by fear or distress or tension, asked something else. Her father replied evenly:

'I've been a lawman a long time and I was an army scout before that. You know it, girl. I read your sign, knew when I was getting close and swung wide of your last night camp down south of Lorenston. Got to White Rock in the middle of the night and hid out in an empty shack at the north end of the street. Waited for you and Buchan to show up.'

Stephenson glanced into the stable as Steele made sounds to encourage the two trail-weary horses to stir. And if he had seen a gun under the Virginian's belt which was not there now, he gave no sign of it. Perhaps because he was too depressed by his own morose mood to see anything except a very general view of his immediate surroundings.

'But why?' Lucy asked. 'What has your daughter's fiancé done?'

Ruth said before her father could reply: 'Stolen his precious daughter who used to cook his meals for him and clean his house for him and launder his clothes. When Frank asked me to marry him, it was too much for my father to take and so he's tried to——'

She broke off as Steele showed at the stable doorway, the bridle of a horse in his left hand, the reins of the other in his right, asked:

'What now?'

'We're going back down the alley and across the street, Mr Steele. To the front of the saloon. It'll haunt me for the rest of my life, but if I have to, I'll shoot Mrs Steele. Shoot anyone who——'

'You won't have to,' Steele told her, gestured for Stephenson to move out of his path and go across the yard ahead of him. Then he followed with the horses and Ruth brought up the rear, steering Lucy with the gun now pressed into the small of her back, which hid it from any casual observers.

If there was anybody watching, they were not out on the street in the blistering heat of the day. Or if anyone looked upon the scene surreptitiously from inside the flanking buildings, they gave no sign of seeing anything unusual as a stranger to town, Steele leading two horses, and Mrs Steele closely followed by another stranger crossed from the mouth of the alley into the front of Bart Dillon's saloon.

As the group came to a halt, a figure emerged from the deep shade in back of the saloon's batwing doors. Was seen to be Frank Buchan as he pushed between the slatted doors, Dillon's elderly Colt clutched in his right hand.

'Mr Stephenson, I warned you not to try and——' Buchan started.

'What happened to Bart Dillon?' Steele asked flatly.

'Tied up and gagged in his own cell,' Buchan answered. He raised his free hand to touch the blood-crusted corner of his mouth, like the sight of Steele reawakened the pain of the punch. 'He never expected somebody like Ruth to snatch his gun.'

'I know how he feels,' Stephenson growled miserably. 'I never expected a daughter of mine to——'

'Let's cut the cackle and get movin'!' Buchan broke in. 'Back off you people, so me and Ruth can get outta this town. Before anyone gets hurt worse than a crack over the head.'

Steele released his hold on the horses, moved away and signalled for his wife to follow. Lucy did so, took hold of his arm and he felt the tension in her that had never for a moment showed while she was under threat from the gun.

The Grover sheriff hesitated for a moment, then backed off to join them.

Ruth swung up into the saddle first, while Buchan kept the group covered. Then she levelled her father's Colt down at them while Buchan got mounted.

Still there was no sound or sign that anyone else in White Rock saw what was taking place and intended to do anything about it.

'And please, Dad,' Ruth said, her tone and expression beseeching him to agree to what she asked, 'don't come after us. Don't try to stop us from being happy. When a daughter gets to be a woman she needs more than a father in her life.'

Stephenson looked sick at heart as he shrugged and nodded. But because his expression was neutral is was impossible to tell if he was leaving the question open, went along with the sentiment.

Then Buchan said something to Ruth that was inaudible to everyone else. And they both thudded in their heels, spurted the barely rested horses into an instant gallop.

'Do me a favour, Steele?' Dwight Stephenson asked as Lucy coughed on more dust raised by pumping hooves and Steele moved a hand in front of his face, could not stop some dust from sticking to his sweat-sheened flesh.

'This really is none of my concern,' the Virginian answered.

'Loan me that pistol you had stuck in your belt awhile back in the stable?'

'Those horses won't make it far at that speed, but I reckon they're out of handgun range already,' Steele said.

But he stooped, hiked up the cuff of his right pants leg and drew Buchan's gun from out where he had lodged it in the side of his boot: close to the place he used to strap on the sheath with a knife in it. When he had carried a knife in this fashion, he always wore pants with a slit seam, so he could draw the weapon fast. In the days before he married and became a small town storekeeper.

'I'm better than most,' Stephenson said, dull toned, as he took the revolver that Steele handed him, butt first.

Maybe fifty yards separated him from the riders, widening by the moment, as he smoothly raised his left arm, crooked it at the elbow and rested the barrel of the revolver across the wrist. Thumbed back the hammer, tilted his head to squint his eye behind the sights. Squeezed the trigger and vented a sound like a sob as his daughter tipped forward in the saddle, leaned to the side, thudded to the ground as her horse raced away.

'Oh, my God!' Lucy gasped, and clung tight to Steele's arm. 'He shot her down!'

'I know the law,' the Grover sheriff said. 'It's the same for all. She's a fugitive, same as he is.'

He cocked the gun again, as Buchan reined in his mount, wheeled the animal toward the woman who was unmoving on the street.

Steele winced as his wife's clawed fingers dug into his arm, said: 'That was some shot with a revolver, feller.'

'I try not to do anythin' I'm not good at,' Stephenson answered as Buchan leapt from his saddle to squat beside Ruth.

'Guess I'm through with being a bad father now.'

Buchan gave a roar of anger and grief, straightened up and went for his stolen gun. It was clear of the holster but not cocked when a bullet from his own revolver took him in the chest. He staggered backward a few paces while he struggled to level the gun, but the shot he fired bit into the ground a few feet in front of him. Then he went down, became spreadeagled on the street a few feet from the woman.

'What did they do?' Lucy asked, her voice taut with shock, her scowl indicating she was primed to condemn the lawman for what he had just done, no matter how he answered.

'Frank Buchan robbed a stage and killed three people,' Stephenson said in a monotone as he lowered the gun but continued to peer fixedly at where he had fired the bullets. 'Stole a couple of hundred dollars.'

'But you shot your daughter!' Lucy insisted, the scowl etching deeper into her face.

The lawman went on in the same toneless voice: 'I was holdin' him for trial in the Grover jail, waitin' for the circuit judge. But Ruth fell for him, helped him escape. Gave him the matched pair of silver plated Remingtons I won for pistol shootin': best shot in all Texas.'

'But——' Lucy attempted to object again.

'He used my guns to shoot down two of my deputies. One killed right off, the other sure to be dead by now. Kinda hopin' my guns are in his saddlebags. But it don't matter for the law: we got plenty of witnesses to the murders. Here, I'm much obliged.'

He turned Buchan's gun, to thrust it butt first back to Steele. But the Virginian shook his head, explained:

'It's not mine, Sheriff. I took it off Frank Buchan.'

He made to start across the street but Lucy maintained her grip on his arm and stood her ground, said:

'Adam, what about poor Mr Dillon? He's still locked up in the cell, tied up and——'

'Like everything else that's happened today,' her husband told her, 'it's none of my concern unless what's mine is threatened. Let those whose business it is take care of what needs to be done, Lucy.'

She started to insist: 'But Adam, you can't just walk away

like this and not——'

'Just watch me,' he told her, tugged free of her restraining hand on his arm and gestured toward the White Rock Grocery. 'These days, that's my business.'

3

About two miles from the place below the hillcrest where the San Francisco and Central California stage was held up and robbed, the Cowley mother and daughter and their three male accomplices angled off the trail through the timber and veered from due south into the south east.

Because of the kind of country, it was not difficult at first for Adam Steele to see and follow their sign. For the isolated nature of the terrain meant it had probably never been trodden by man or horse before. So there was a hundred per cent certainty that every recently snapped twig, each hoofmark in turf, discarded butt, dead match and horse apple was left by the people he was tracking.

But when afternoon gave way to evening, twilight came early to the sloping floor of the mountain forest and the sign of his quarry's passing became less easy to spot. So the Virginian had a decision to make, based upon certain educated guesses.

They did not know they were being followed. Maybe at the start they had considered the possibility, purposely strewn their backtracks with sign to lure an unwary tracker into a trap. But such a trap would have been sprung long ago. Later, carelessness born of confidence was why they did not trouble to cover their sign, which included evidence of a cold meal they ate in a rocky glade.

That had made Steele grimly aware of his own hunger, caused him to speed up his pursuit: sometimes on horseback, often having to lead the gelding by the reins or bridle. Frequently veering from side to side as he followed the two women and three men who took the only available way around some obstacles or elected by luck or good judgement to take the least difficult of two routes when another option was to go back.

Sometimes they had been forced to turn around and try

again. And this enabled Steele to close the gap on them, for invariably he was able to spot the backtracking sign early: avoid making the same mistakes as they made by pressing forward toward an eventual dead end.

In addition to being sure they were unaware of being followed, Steele reached another conclusion about his quarry. Despite how rocky escarpments and dense stands of timber caused the route to snake, it invariably led back on to a generally south eastern direction. Drew him higher into the Sierra Nevadas in a manner that suggested at least one member of the bunch of road agents knew where they were headed. But had never approached the ultimate destination from this direction before.

Previously had held up stages on different stretches of the trail before making off for their hide-out in the hills, Steele reflected sardonically as he was finally forced to abandon the search for signs in the gathering gloom. Had to decide whether to rest up for the night and start out at first light tomorrow, or to keep going on an assumption based upon another educated guess.

Like because they were unable to plot their course by dead reckoning, they were finding their way through this rugged terrain by heading for a distinctive feature on one of the high ridges of the Sierra Nevadas.

There were many such features, but Steele had taken particular notice of a snow-covered crag dotted with outcrops of rock that showed black against the snow to form the rough shape of an old man's face. Often during the day the crag had been hidden by intervening trees and hillcrests. But it always came into view again, never too far to the left or right of dead ahead.

The Cowley women and Daryl, Ricky and Mel were not aiming to go to the crag. From when Steele had last seen it, it was at least thirty miles distant and maybe three thousand feet higher than his position. But it certainly looked like the landmark that was keeping them on course for where they were headed.

Trouble was, he could not see it after the final traces of the sunset had disappeared and left the sky and timbered landscape inky black. So it seemed he had no option but to stay put until

71

the first light of a new day's dawn.

But then, just as he was through fashioning a bed for himself out of dry pine needles dragged into an elongated heap, the moon rose and lit an area of sky that had previously been darkened. And its glittering light struck the distant high ridge in such a way that the man's face seemed to be grinning down at him through the treetops.

Steele did not believe in charms, omens or strokes of luck . . . well, not often, anyway. But because the highly prized Colt Hartford had been stolen, and the thieves intended to remove the inscribed gold plate that made the rifle so special to him, he was willing to grasp at any straw.

The horse from out of the stage team tried to warn him against what he intended to do. Or was that in the same realm of the unreal as belief in luck? Whatever, as soon as the gelding realised they were going to push on through the night, he gave a loud and prolonged snort of disgust that seemed to carry far enough through the timbered mountainscape to hit the distant, face-shaped ridge. Against which it echoed with a sound like the old man sculptured there was laughing.

The complaint registered, the animal that had been well behaved since submitting to the will of the man quietened again. Was as docile as a saddle-broken old mare when Steele gripped the bridle to lead him away from the intended night camp. This while Steele himself had to make a conscious effort to contain his anger as he struggled to tear from his mind an almost painful image of the plate being prised off the rosewood stock of his rifle.

In part the degree of anger he felt was from a sense of loss over the stolen Colt Hartford: but it was made worse because he knew that a man in his position, owner of a fine horse ranch on a prime piece of California land, was pretty damn stupid to get so emotional about a gun.

A special rifle, sure: because it was the sole inheritance from his father. But he should surely by now have acknowledged that the old life was gone for ever. The compromise had been made and it was crazy to be risking his life for the sake of a final link with the ancient past.

Which was what he was doing, for he sure as hell was not chasing a bunch of road agents up this mountain for the seven and a half bucks he had surrendered to them. Nor did he have a pressing need for the thousand dollar reward Alvin Townsend had put up for the return of his wife's jewellery.

No, this crazy trek—which got even crazier as he started to press on virtually blind through the night—was on account of that special rifle.

Then, when he finally acknowledged that no matter how much he tried to talk himself out of it, the rifle always would mean a great deal to him, his anger immediately cooled. And as this happened, he became abruptly aware of the physical cold that was affecting him.

He was well below the snowline, but considerably higher than the point where the stage was held up. Higher than anywhere on the trail between San Francisco and Providence. So he was wearing only the city suit he had considered adequate for the stage ride between the two towns, and suitable for his business dealings in Frisco: a suit which, along with the other clothing he had on, was designed for style rather than to keep out high mountain night cold.

He jammed his hat down harder on his head and turned up the collar of his jacket, but the impression of warmth this created endured just a few seconds. Pushing one buckskin-gloved hand at a time into a pocket while the other held the bridle made the rest of his body feel colder by contrast.

He never got on the back of the horse, to risk the animal stumbling and throwing him. Or being hit in the face by a low branch that might pitch him to the ground with equally painful and dangerous results. And, much as it irked him to walk, particularly on an almost constant upslope, at least the exercise served to keep the blood pumping through his veins which surely helped him to keep warm.

Because he had gradually gained height since he left the trail, the timber had gotten sparser and in his present impressionable mood, it felt like the air got colder: like the trees emanated a kind of warmth. Also, it seemed the colder the air, the thinner and more difficult to breathe it became.

Sometimes he felt hungry, but he still had the presence of mind not to be concerned about this: he knew he was in greater danger of freezing to death than starving.

Even more likely, his end would come from a bullet fired by

one of the bunch he was following. For as the timber thinned, so the field of view for a look-out got deeper and wider. And without the muffling effect of close growing trees up here, much less obtrusive sounds than the snort of the horse would carry much further. In reality: not just imagination.

Reality: that was what it was important he should cling to.

Cold and hunger did not cause a man to see the same kind of mirages as heat and thirst: but from past experience he knew their effect could be just as dangerous. And with the degree of weariness he was starting to feel from the long climb, it would be all too easy to submit to the demands of his body that he rest. Persuade him to find a sheltered place in the rocks or under a thicket of brush in which to conjure up an impression of snugness. Curl up, let sleep overtake him: but the kind of sleep that might turn out to be his longest and last.

Because he worked so hard to keep a grip on reality, refused to allow into his mind the merest notion that signalled he was letting his imagination run away with him he did not immediately acknowledge the scent of smoke in the air. For smoke indicated fire, and fire was warming. Therefore an impression of woodsmoke tainting the previously clear and clean mountain air was likely to be a kind of mirage created by cold.

Then the horse vented a nervous snort and tossed his head. Which was maybe an instinctive equine reaction out of fear of fire.

Steele stopped then, sucked in a stream of cold, thin mountain air. Which was definitely permeated with wood-smoke. Not strongly, so either the fire was a considerable distance away or nearby and almost out.

He looked and listened intently as he stood on the brightly moonlit and darkly moon-shadowed expanse of hillside where tall, meagre pines were widely spaced over ground that was more rocky than grassed now.

Directly ahead, looking no closer than when he saw it in the light of the newly risen moon, was the snowy ridge which had guided him this far. But it was closer, of course, and viewed from this angle it no longer resembled an old man's face. Now it simply looked like a partially snow-covered mountain ridge.

But it was the same high point he had been using as a marker, he was sure of that. Because, damnit, he had hardly ever taken his eyes off it. Probably this as much as the other factors had put him in danger of losing touch with reality so often.

But no more.

He now saw smoke ahead and to the right. Hanging above what looked from where he stood like the top of a cliff where the upward sloping ground suddenly ended. Not much smoke. Like it was from a small fire disturbed by a stray draught or maybe somebody had stirred the almost dead ashes to uncover a few glowing embers. Even as he watched, it vanished in the surrounding air.

The horse quivered, but did not make any sound. Submitted tamely to having the reins hitched to some low brush, before Steele moved cautiously away, advancing on the top of the slope along a zig-zag path from tree to tree.

He reasoned that if anyone was in a postion to watch the slope they would already have spotted him. He did not think this was so: but he needed the scant cover of the trees because there was a danger a pebble could roll, a dry twig crack or the part-broken in horse might be spooked into a whinney. And he did not know how far below the top of the slope the fire was, if it was attended by an alert sentry.

But why wasn't such a sentry posted on the high ground, positioned to see a pursuer before he got this close?

Because he was posted to guard against a threat from another direction?

Hell, that didn't make any sense—yet.

As Steele, almost at the crest, was about to advance from behind the relative safety of a spindly pine, somebody said something. He crouched and froze in mid-stride. And for stretched seconds was unsure if he had actually heard a voice.

Then a response was made and there was no doubt this time. A man had certainly said something, but the Virginian was unable to discern what it was. For the soft-spoken words were in a foreign language. The sense of what was said was incomprehensible, yet there was something familiar about the oddly guttural yet melodic tones of the voice.

Damnit, they were talking an Indian dialect!

He started forward again, anxious but at the same time relieved by this new factor in the pursuit. He would really be crazy to be complacent about the possibility of a run in with a bunch of redskins. But it was a weight off his mind to know they were unaware of his presence because they had no reason to expect him to be there. Which explained why they were camped at the base of this sheer-faced, fifty-feet-high cliff. He bellied into a position to see down.

There were ten of them, two sitting tightly wrapped in blankets beside the almost dead fire while the other eight were peacefully asleep nearby. Some rifles, pouches, canteens and other belongings were stowed in an untidy heap. But if the braves had any ponies the animals were not tethered close by the campsite.

Steele peered down at the night camp for several seconds, waiting for further talk that might signal some sort of action. But whatever had been asked and answered had served the purpose of the two braves for the moment.

And he switched his attention to what was surely the reason the Indians were in this particular place right then.

Perhaps a mile away along the shallow, virtually treeless valley at the western head of which they were camped was a stone building surrounded by a stockade fence. On two sides of the single storey building the fence had partially collapsed from the passage of time, the assault of the elements or the destructive actions of mankind. But from this distance the building looked to be in a much better state of repair and Steele found himself wondering if the people inside felt safe and secure within the shelter of the sound walls and solid roof.

Wondered if there were five people, not just three as might be suggested by that number of horses he could see. Wondered if they were Thelma and Belle Cowley, Daryl, Ricky and Mel. Wondered just what the Indians had in mind for those people, whoever they were.

Which was a lot of wondering for a man physically weary and emotionally drained: but who was able to smile as he withdrew from his vantage point and returned to the horse, said softly as he stroked the animal's neck:

'You were right, feller. Where there's smoke there's fire. I just hope I pull out my favourite shooting iron.'

The Troublemakers

At the conclusion of *Wagons East* Adam Steele rode out of the town of Oakdale, Oregon. When he showed up in the next book of the series, *The Big Game*, he was in Chicago, Illinois. There are a lot of miles between the two towns and as he rode the long trail the Virginian's journey was not without incident.

The noise and dust of the herd's entry into town had subsided and the single street of Newville, Kansas, was quiet again in the unobstructed glare of the mid-afternoon sun for perhaps a full minute. Then doors and windows were re-opened and houseproud women and fastidious storekeepers emerged to sweep their stoops and the sidewalks out front of their premises.

Few sounds of this cleaning campaign reached into the Trail's End saloon, for it was isolated by several vacant lots from its nearest neighbour at the southern end of the street.

The regular tick of the clock on the wall behind the bar counter was the only sound loud enough to be heard within the saloon until the whore in the red dress said:

'Gonna be a heavy night tonight, Baker.'

The bartender, who had no stoop or sidewalk to sweep and was uncaring about the dust which had floated in through the batwinged entrance, did not look up from the mail order catalogue he was studying when he growled: 'We could sure use the business.'

'Speak for yourself, Baker,' the whore in the green dress rasped. 'Where the lousy Double Bar bunch is concerned.'

The bartender said dismissively: 'Charlie Brewster always pays for the breakages his boys leave behind them.'

'Ain't no money can repay the damage that bunch say they'd do to us!' the green-gowned whore countered sourly.

'Shit, that was all just liquor talk, Charlene,' the whore in the red dress said, her tone bored. Then she smiled brightly, her manner suddenly friendly, as a man came down the stairway at the far end of the bar counter. 'Hello again, Mr Steele. Noise of the herd hittin' town wake you up?'

'No, ma'am, I just slept until I'd had enough,' the Virginian drawled.

'And you still don't have no need of any special services?' Charlene asked, trying to make her smile more alluring than that spread across the over-painted face of the other woman.

'No, ma'am. Just need a cup of coffee.'

Baker grunted scornfully as he looked up from the catalogue, complained: 'That's a special service in a saloon, mister. Any other man comes into the Trail's End, he drinks liquor or he drinks beer.'

'I'm not any other man, feller,' Steele replied evenly.

'You can say that again,' Baker muttered as he pushed through a bead-curtained archway into the back of his place.

Steele went to a table on the far side of the saloon from the two women who looked older than their years. Sat on a chair with his back to the wall against which he leaned the Colt Hartford.

He certainly was not anything like the middle-aged, heavily built, balding and unshaven Baker. Nor was it likely he had much in common with anyone else he had so far seen in this small town.

Steele was just on the right side of forty, just a shade over five and a half feet tall and built on lean lines that belied his strength.

He was dressed like a dude who had been down on his luck for some time: which was about true. Wore a once-stylish, once-pale blue city suit that was now heavily soiled by trail dust. Beneath was a purple vest with some of its buttons missing and a lace-trimmed white shirt that was both dirty and torn. His Stetson was grey and had cost a lot of money a long time ago.

At odds with the dudish clothing was a pair of scuffed black buckskin gloves on his hands and a sweat-stained silken scarf around his throat. Even had every part of his outfit been newly purchased, these items would have struck wrong notes.

78

'One pot of coffee, mister,' Baker announced resentfully as he came through the arch and set down the pot and a mug on the bar counter. 'And some advice: at no extra charge.'

'Grateful for the coffee,' the Virginian said as he went to collect his order. 'And I'll listen to the advice, though I won't promise to take it.'

Baker waited until Steele returned to the table and sat down. Then as the coffee was poured from pot to mug, he warned:

'Don't be in here when the Double Bar boys come by tonight.'

Steele nodded. 'I heard.'

Baker asked quickly: 'What d'you hear, mister?'

'The advice.'

Baker snorted, rasped the back of a hand along his bristled jawline, explained: 'Look, it's for your own good. Newville ain't got much for the Texans who bring their critters up the trail from the south, eatin' dust every stinkin' step of the way. Just the liquor and the beer and the girls.'

'Every man to his taste, feller.'

Baker pressed on: 'Usually when they've had their fill of them, they start in to card playin'.'

Steele shrugged. 'Enjoy a hand or two of cards myself, on occasion.'

'Most times, they finish up fightin',' Baker said. 'Each other.'

'It happens, feller.'

'Sure it happens. It could also happen that a man like you could turn out to be an added attraction for them Texans.'

'I could?'

'Sure! On account of them saddlebums ain't never seen nothin' like you in this town before. And maybe not anywhere before.'

'Grateful to you.'

'I don't want your gratitude, damnit!' Baker snarled, spraying spittle in his rising anger. 'I just want you to be gone before they show up in my place tonight!'

'I checked in for today and tonight!'

Baker compressed his lips, maybe counted a good way to ten. Then allowed in a more controlled tone: 'I know it. So okay. Just keep to your room? You in your fancy threads and totin' that fancy rifle. Keep yourself hid away from them

79

hell-raisin', itchin'-to-make-trouble Texans. Especially the Double Bar bunch this trip.'

Steele took a long drink of the strong, black coffee, then said: 'Feller?'

'Yeah?'

'Don't tell me what to do.'

Steele's voice still had a soft Virginian drawl, but there was now an ice coldness discernible in back of it.

The two whores had started in to play a no-stakes game of five card draw. As Baker shook his head and spread a scowl across his darkly bristled face, the one dressed in red rasped:

'Baker's givin' you good advice, dude!'

Steele blew across the steaming surface of the coffee in the mug, answered: 'Yeah, I told him I was grateful.'

Later that day the Double Bar herd arrived in Newville, Sheriff Bill Foster stepped outside of his office and peered northward along the town's only street to where, beyond the railroad depot and the crowded stock holding pens, the Texas outfit was camped.

Foster was a big man, an inch over six feet tall and weighing in the region of two hundred and ten pounds, little of it excess fat, as could be seen from the way his blue denim pants and grey shirt with a star pinned to the left pocket fitted his frame so snugly. He was thirty-two years old.

As he gazed out across the railroad tracks that marked Newville's northern limit, his square face, narrow-eyed and firm-jawed, wore an expression of menace. He expected trouble from the newly arrived cowpunchers and was ready, willing and able to use his muscular frame in dealing with it.

He did not wear a gunbelt, and during the seven years he had been a lawman in Kansas railroad towns he never had done so.

As the afternoon light faded and evening waited for the sun to sink far out across the prairie, though, Foster was having doubts about whether he could handle the trouble that threatened the town on this particular night.

The punchers who brought the Longhorn herds up from Texas had not always camped outside Newville town limits. In the old days, before the town council hired Foster to keep the peace in this community, the Texans had stayed in town. At the Trail's End saloon, in Ma Dunne's boarding house, in rooms

80

rented by several citizens or in an alleyway or under any piece of sidewalk where the more liquored-up happened to collapse.

Which had led to far too much trouble spread over too long a time. And the hell that was raised left in its wake too much damage. Gave Newville a bad reputation in times that were changing.

So the former sheriff was fired and Bill Foster was hired on. Soon proved his fame for cleaning up towns was well founded. In this instance restricted the time the cowpunchers could stay within Newville town limits between the hours of six in the evening and midnight.

The idea was simple enough, but it had caused trouble with a number of outfits over the last year. Threats had been voiced and some were carried out. Punches were thrown, guns fired and some blood spilled, assorted bones broken. But nobody had gotten killed and the heavy fines imposed were all paid.

The Texans and those citizens of Newville who resented Bill Foster's methods finally got the message. When a herd was in the holding pens, waiting for the Chicago-bound train, men and women who wanted no truck with the punchers could sleep peacefully in their beds and go about their respectable business without hindrance between the hours of midnight and six the following evening.

Those who wanted the company or the money of the free-wheeling and high-spending trail herders had merely to be on the street or keep their premises open from six to midnight.

They had, of course, to accept the consequences: for they had no resort to the law in the shape of Sheriff Bill Foster. Who, as an honest and dedicated peace officer, was not entirely satisfied with the situation he had created.

But, he reminded himself again, so far nobody had gotten themselves killed. But with the Double Bar outfit back in town, tonight could be different. And if some citizen who chose to mix with the cowhands was killed, how could he shelter behind the contention that it was the victim's own stupid fault?

The clock on the courthouse tower began to strike the hour of six. And Foster spat a globule of saliva into the dusty street before he swung around and went back inside his office.

The area where the cowpunchers were required to stay during the off-limits periods was not so much a camp as a sort

81

of hotel. Sited to one side of the north trail, it comprised a bunkhouse, a stable, a building with cooking and eating facilities and a bath house. Most men agreed it was more comfortable and cleaner than a lot of the places in town and back at the spreads where the outfits came from.

Most of the men who stayed there came to appreciate it. Even the majority of Double Bar hands were content in surroundings which offered the opportunity to wash up and rest after gruelling weeks on the trail, to prepare for a night on the town and afterwards to sleep off the effects. But not all.

'It ain't got no walls around it and it's a hell of a lot fancier, but it's still a damn prison,' Floyd Boyer growled.

'Sure is,' Pat Flannigan agreed.

'What we gonna do about it?' Frank Lincoln wanted to know.

'What we told that sonofabitchin' lawman we would,' Wayne Ritchie answered as the other three looked quizzically at him.

It was a little after seven o'clock and the quartet of Texans had the long bunkhouse to themselves. They were sprawled out on their backs at one end of the building, freshly bathed and shaved and fully dressed.

All were in their late twenties, tall and muscular, bodies hardened by the tough job they did and skin darkened and cracked by the harsh mixture of weathers in which they often had to work.

'We warned Foster we'd get him as I recall, Wayne,' the blond-haired Flannigan reminded, 'that's all.'

'You ain't said how we're gonna do that.' This from the prematurely balding, bushily moustached Lincoln.

As Ritchie folded up from the bunk and swung his feet to the floor, the squint-eyed Boyer said: 'But I figure you thought of something, uh?'

'You bet your asses, old buddies,' Ritchie crowed, and vented a loud laugh that puckered the scar of an old knife wound which extended from the top of his right sideburn to the corner of his mouth. Then he ended the sound abruptly and his expression became as grim as his tone when he explained his plan to the other three.

'Mr Brewster won't like it, Wayne,' Flannigan warned

anxiously when Ritchie was through with the explanation.

'Then Charlie Brewster can do the other thing, right old buddy?' Ritchie rasped between clenched teeth as he knotted the laces to hold the toe of his holster snug to his right thigh.

'Damn right,' Boyer growled eagerly.

Lincoln urged: 'Let's get to it!'

While four of his men were setting out to teach Sheriff Bill Foster a lesson, the grey-bearded Charlie Brewster, who at over fifty was still considered to be one of the hardest and meanest and best trail bosses in the cattle business, was playing the out-of-tune piano in the saloon.

Short and solidly built, with a wrinkled face and piercingly blue eyes, Brewster had gnarled hands that looked well suited to heavy work but incapable of gentleness. Yet when his working day was over he enjoyed nothing better than to play guitar or piano: surprisingly well.

In the Trail's End tonight only one listener appeared to be appreciating his musicianship. The slightly built, dudishly dressed man who sat alone at a table on the other side of the saloon from where Brewster was playing.

His name was Adam Steele, Baker had told Brewster in response to the trail boss's direct enquiry. He had walked into town this morning with his gear over a shoulder and asked at the depot when the next train for Chicago was scheduled. When he was informed this would not be until noon the next day, he had checked into the Trail's End.

In answer to a question from the whore named Susan, Steele had volunteered the information that his horse went lame five miles west of town. He had shot the animal and walked the rest of the way into Newville. He drank only coffee, had no yen for Susan or Charlene and did not invite conversation. Nothing else was known about him.

Brewster, who was able to glance surreptitiously across the saloon without interrupting his piano playing, decided he did not trust the man. Who took a long time to drink a mug of coffee while he was engaged in a game of solitaire. Seemingly totally detached from all that was happening around him. Except the music, because he beat time on the tabletop with the fingertips of a gloved hand every now and then.

Brewster did not trust him because Steele carried no visible handgun: yet virtually flaunted the fancy sporting rifle which at the moment leaned against the wall within easy reach. Like a challenge: inviting trouble.

And Charlie Brewster was aware that some of his men were looking for trouble tonight, so as he continued to play a sweetly melancholy melody the bearded man directed another glance across the saloon. Then around it. Saw Adam Steele was dealing out the cards for another lonesome game, while a couple of more social card games were still in progress: one stud and the other draw poker. One of them among five Double Bar hands, the other engaging the attentions of two of his boys and two Newville storekeepers. A dozen assorted cowhands and local citizens were bellied up to the bar counter and a line of five Double Bar men were waiting at the foot of the stairway to take their turn with Charlene and Susan.

Everyone in the place except for Steele, the bartender and Brewster was drinking. Most were smoking. There was a great deal of loud talk and frequent gusts of laughter. It seemed like a good saloon atmosphere, with nothing to portend trouble. But Brewster remained uneasy.

Sheriff Bill Foster had not yet looked in on the Trail's End.

And Wayne Ritchie and his three closest buddies were nowhere to be seen. But a number of the Newville stores were still open. And other women than the Trail's End whores sometimes made themselves available: a trio of youngish widows and the unmarried daughter of the local blacksmith among them.

Maybe Ritchie and his pals had been all talk. Maybe they were trying their luck elsewhere in town. Or were out buying some essentials for the ride back home, some trinkets for the girls they left behind them. They would drift in later, get drunk and go with the whores if they had failed with the other approachable women of the town. The whole Double Bar bunch would get roaring drunk, and after a real or imagined wrong, the fighting would start. At midnight they would head noisily back up the street and over the railroad tracks, all certain they'd had a good time.

And Baker and Brewster would assess the damage and reach an agreement on the cost to cover it. Tomorrow Brewster would pay for the breakages out of the money for the sale of the herd. And when the steers were safely loaded on the east-bound train, the whole outfit would ride on out down the trail toward Texas.

Anyway, that's how it would be in a world as near perfect as Charlie Brewster had any right to expect. And when he broke off from the sad melody and started on a more tuneful one he tried to pretend it reflected his mood. But an anxiety in his eyes belied this. He was still uneasy about the damn dude!

Adam Steele knew of the interest Charlie Brewster showed. He was also aware that most of the steadily drinking cowpunchers who were bossed by the bearded man were curious about him. But he was used to being considered somewhat odd, sometimes thought of as a figure of fun, because he did not dress like most people did in frontier towns. Did not enjoy what they enjoyed. Did not pack a sixshooter in a holster. Chose to tote a Colt Hartford revolver action sporting rifle instead of the popular Winchester.

But he showed no sign of resentment or even discomfiture as he went on playing games of solitaire, losing out more often than he won against the cards. He left his chair only once, to go back to the latrine. He took the rifle with him, drawing mass attention toward him, which he ignored.

A minute or so later Sheriff Bill Foster pushed in between the batwings, raked a wary-eyed gaze over the occupants of the crowded saloon.

Talk was stilled, Brewster ended the music and Baker growled:

'Everythin's fine, Bill.'

'Pleased to hear it, Burt,' the lawman replied as he crossed to the bar counter. 'But I came in for a beer, is all.'

'Comin' right up.'

Talk and the card games restarted, but Brewster gave up on the piano, went to the bar to order a beer for himself. From there he was better able to keep a watchful eye on Steele. And Foster when the lawman sat down at the dude's table.

'Buy you a drink, stranger?'

'Gave it up a long time ago, Sheriff.'

Foster shrugged. 'Did Burt Baker warn you there'll likely be some trouble later?'

Steele showed the kind of boyish smile that seemed to take

several years off his age. 'He reckoned I should hide in my room.'

Foster did not smile as he said: 'Sound advice.'

Steele continued with his solo game of cards as he answered evenly: 'He claimed it was advice and it sounded like advice. I told him not to tell me what I should do.'

'How about if you just stowed that rifle in your room?'

'You asking me or telling me, Sheriff?'

'Uh?'

'If the first, the answer is no. If the second—and you insist—there's certain to be trouble. Sooner rather than later.'

Foster's expression hardened. 'Tough nut, uh?'

'If the need arises, Sheriff.'

The lawman finished his beer at a swallow and nodded. 'My guess is that'll be just before midnight. When this bunch have got themselves liquored-up enough to need a little more excitement than Charlene or Susan can provide.'

'The bartender said so.'

'Just don't get tough enough to use that rifle, mister. Or any other fancy gun you got tucked up your sleeve or wherever. I'll not tolerate killing in this town.'

Steele nodded, said: 'It's your job not to, feller.'

Foster rose, turned and went out of the saloon. All eyes except those of the Virginian tracked the sheriff's exit. Then, as the batwings flapped closed behind the lawman, attention was switched back to Steele. And since nobody had been close enough to overhear the two men's conversation, suspicion was now mixed in with curiosity.

'Another pot of coffee, bartender?' Steele asked.

'How the hell you ever get to sleep at nights, mister?' Baker growled.

'I put it down to having a clear conscience, feller.'

'And he wakes up with a clear head,' a Double Bar hand muttered bitterly in the soured voice of being already drunk beyond the best stage, beginning to anticipate the hangover he would suffer in the morning.

Brewster shot a fast, hard glance at the man, concerned he was about to spark trouble. But the drunken cowpuncher felt no resentment toward the dude as he rose and staggered to join the line waiting for the whores.

Later, as the hour of eight started to be struck by the clock on the courthouse tower, Baker delivered a pot of fresh coffee to Adam Steele's table. And a man on the street yelled:

'Fire! Hey, Sheriff! The camp's on fire!'

Inside the saloon there was a started paused, then a man blurted:

'Hey, that sounds like Wayne Ritchie!'

'Yeah, it is!' Brewster snarled.

Men whirled from the bar counter and sprang up from chairs that tipped over. All headed for the doorway.

'You Double Bar boys!' Wayne Ritchie yelled. 'Get the hell on out here and down to the camp! We could lose all our damn gear!'

He continued to shout, but the rest of what he said was lost behind the barrage of other raised voices inside the saloon and out on the street. Plus the racket raised by the penned herd of Longhorns in fearful response to the sudden din and the smell of smoke.

Within moments, Adam Steele was sitting alone in the Trail's End saloon. Until two men who had been with the whores clattered down the stairway and across the saloon, cursing as they fastened their belt buckles. The batwings flapped closed behind them, the sound loud now the crowd noises had receded to the far north end of the street.

Steele started to pour himself a mug of coffee and had company again, when the two whores hurried down the stairway.

'Ain't you comin' to see the fire?' Susan in the red dress asked, breathless with excitement.

'You fool around with that, you can get burned, ma'am,' he said.

Charlene in the green dress accused sourly: 'It might warm you up some!'

Then they both plunged out on to the street and as the thud of their running footfalls diminished, Steele picked up the full mug of coffee and reached for the rifle, intending to go up to his room. He reasoned that with trouble concentrated in the other side of town, the saloon would be quiet from now on and he could get a night of uninterrupted sleep.

But a man ordered: 'Leave it where it is!'

Steele froze as he recognised the voice of the man: knew it was the same one that had sounded the fire alarm.

'Who the hell are you?'

'A feller minding his own business.'

Wayne Ritchie stepped between the batwings, a cocked Remington in his rock-steady right hand aimed at the Virginian. There was a mixture of anger and puzzlement on his knife-scarred face as he demanded: 'Why ain't you at the fire?'

'That's not my business.'

'The whole damn town's supposed to go out to the camp!' Ritchie insisted, sounding suddenly like a spoiled child denied his own way.

Then Steele could see from the man's face that countless notions rushed through his mind, each to be momentarily considered and rejected. But he finally reached a decision.

Then, as he came away from the batwings, the revolver never wavering in its aim at Steele, Boyer, Flannigan and Lincoln burst into the saloon behind him. Each carried a bulging gunnysack.

They halted, stared blankly at Steele as Ritchie went behind the bar counter, jerked out the cash drawer and emptied its contents on the bartop. Some of the bills and coins spilled to the floor, but most stayed there.

The trio at the doorway had been grinning before their faces went blank. Now fear gripped them as they flicked their gazes between Ritchie and Steele.

'What the hell's happenin', Wayne?' the squint-eyed man asked.

'Who's he?' the prematurely bald one demanded.

'Shit, the whole thing's gone wrong!' the blond complained.

The scar-faced man behind the counter showed a brutal grin as he corrected: 'Nah, it's gonna be even better than I planned it, old buddies. Bring that money over here. Put it all in one sack. This, too.' He waved his free hand over the bills and coins from the saloon's cash drawer.

'Well, let us in on it, for frig sake!' Lincoln snarled as he thudded his sack on the counter, held it open for the other two to transfer the contents of their sacks to it.

Ritchie crowed: 'We'll all be heroes! The dude here will be

the patsy instead of that sonofabitchin' Foster! When he wakes up from the lump I gave him, he'll figure it was this guy slugged him.'

'Shit!' Flannigan exclaimed.

Boyer growled: 'I ain't so sure, Wayne.'

'He won't be able to figure it out any other way, good buddies. Not after I tell him how we spotted the dude robbin' the stores while all the other folks was helpin' to fight the fire at the camp. How we trailed him here and got the drop on him.'

Boyer, Flannigan and Lincoln had listened with mounting enthusiasm to Ritchie. Then the moustached Lincoln said eagerly:

'I'll get that rifle of his.'

He was careful to stay out of the line of fire of the Remington as he approached Steele's table.

The Virginian remained impassive, seemingly as coolly unconcerned as he had been all the while since Ritchie first entered the Trail's End.

Thus, when the rifle was claimed by the nervously scowling Lincoln, Steele was able to reach down, appear to scratch the outside of his right calf without the Double Bar hands thinking anything of the gesture. They could not know there was a slit in the seam of the dude's pants which provided access to the knife in the boot sheath.

But the squint-eyed Boyer did find himself provoked to ask anxiously: 'Why ain't he scared, Wayne?'

Ritchie answered with heavy menace: 'I guess because he's too dumb to figure out what's happenin' to him. He's gonna be scared now, though. Pass me that rifle, Frank.'

'What you gonna do?' Lincoln wanted to know, a catch in his voice, as he gave the rifle to the other man.

Still covering Steele with the revolver, Ritchie rested the Colt Hartford across the counter top, thumbed back the hammer.

From the threshold of the saloon, Charlie Brewster demanded thickly: 'What are the whole crazy bunch of you doin'?'

'Even friggin' better!' Ritchie murmured, swung the rifle and squeezed the trigger, laughed.

The bullet from the rifle muzzle cracked across the saloon, blasted a hole in one of the door slats, drove deep into the chest of the Double Bar's trail boss.

Pat Flannigan shrieked: 'There wasn't gonna be no killin'!'

For a full second Brewster stayed on his feet, his expression changing from anger to deep sadness. His big hands were hooked over the tops of the doors as he struggled to remain erect. Then his blue eyes snapped closed and he fell forward. The batwings folded open as his hands dropped off the doors and he sprawled face down across the threshold.

The four cowpunchers stared at the shot man with deep shock, the one who impulsively fired the bullet so gleefully as affected by its result as his partners.

Even before Brewster had started to fall, Adam Steele was on his feet in a half crouch, the knife drawn from the boot sheath, right arm swinging. And now Ritchie looked at him as the knife was released from the gloved hand.

The Virginian lunged in the wake of the spinning blade and the big Texan had no time to bring his revolver back to aim. Or cock the rifle with black powder smoke wisping from its muzzle. Before the knife thudded into his shoulder.

He lurched into a half turn, then was driven to the floor by a flying tackle as Steele launched himself across the bar counter: one hand fisted around the barrel of the Colt Hartford as the other smashed into Ritchie's jaw.

Boyer, Lincoln and Flannigan reacted in unison as they recovered from the shock of the shooting. All went for their holstered revolvers as both Steele and the instantly unconscious Ritchie hit the floor behind the counter.

'One shot and I'll kill your partner!' the Virginian snarled.

He jerked the knife out of the bloodsquirting wound and thumbed back the rifle hammer as he rose on his haunches, showed his head above the counter top.

'Let's go bring the boys!' Boyer snapped.

'Back on out,' Lincoln advised. 'Keep your irons aimed at him.'

Flannigan vented a squeal of horror as he stepped on one of Charlie Brewster's hands. Steele was sure he could have risen, swung the rifle and dropped all three men while they were distracted.

But he did not straighten up until the batwings flapped shut after the cowpunchers went out. And then he looked bleakly down at Wayne Ritchie as he wiped the blood from the knife blade on to the money-filled gunnysack, said: 'Cattle are your business, feller. You shouldn't have messed in mine.'

The shouts of the unconscious man's three partners began to sound on the street as Steele left the Trail's End by the rear door.

The fire at the camp was confined to the building that housed the cookhouse and eating hall. While the Double Bar hands had calmed the panicked steers in the pens, the able-bodied citizens of Newville formed a human chain to bring bucket after bucket of water to hurl on the flames that were quickly brought under control.

Steers and people became less raucously noisy as the flames died down, so the shouts of the three men running up the moonlit street from the saloon were heard before they covered half the distance.

And the crowd turned toward them, abandoned the smouldering ruins of the building and the uneasy Longhorns, attention captured by key words they could pick out of the competing explanations yelled at them.

'... killed ... saloon ... rifle ... dude ... Brewster ... money ... stolen.'

Within two minutes the northern end of the the street was deserted and the confused crowd, bubbling with fear and excitement, gathered out front of the saloon at the southern end.

A man broke from the crowd, ran to the sheriff's office, hurried back moments later, shouting that the lawman was not there.

Out at the camp beyond the railroad depot and holding pens, Steele emerged from around a corner of the undamaged bunkhouse and said: 'You smell it, too, Sheriff?'

Bill Foster stood close to the charred, still smoking shell of the burnt out building. He recognised Steele's voice before he turned and saw in the light of the moon that the Virginian had the Colt Hartford canted to his right shoulder. The lawman gently massaged the side of his head, winced when he answered:

'Yeah. Somebody sure got careless with a lot of kerosene, uh?'

'Ritchie and his three sidekicks, Sheriff.'

Foster nodded, unsurprised by the revelation as, at the other end of the street, a barrage of gunfire exploded. The bullets thudded into timber, shattered window glass.

'They must think I'm still in the saloon,' Steele said as the steers started to snort and scrape at the ground with their hooves, reared and banged against the pen sides.

'What else do you know, Steele?'

The Virginian quickly told the lawman of the plan to frame him for robbery after setting light to the camp building as a diversion. And how Ritchie shot down Charlie Brewster and intended to switch his plan halfway through.

'You know something?' Foster said when Steele was finished. And there was another burst of gunfire from down the street as the Double Bar hands rushed the Trail's End: the penned steers started to act up again.

'There has to be more to it than that,' the Virginian answered.

'Yeah, Ritchie switched his plan too quick and easy. He didn't care who took the blame.'

It was quiet at the far end of the street now. The Double Bar hands were inside the saloon and the citizens of Newville waited nervously out front of the place to hear what they found.

Foster started toward Steele, went on by him.

The Virginian asked: 'Where you headed without a gun, feller?'

The lawman paused and looked back, said grimly: 'Stay out of this, stranger. Law's been broken and I'm the lawman hereabouts.' He massaged the lump on his head again, soured his tone even more to add: 'I've got a personal interest in this trouble, too. The kind that makes me real sore.'

'Bullets will hurt worse.'

Foster ignored the warning, moved inexorably away from the malodorous camp where the night air was still strong with the stinks of old burning. He strode out beyond the end of the railroad depot, across the tracks and was alongside the pens before he was spotted.

'Bill, where the hell you been?' Burt Baker yelled, anger mixed in with relief at seeing the familiar figure.

The crowd made to move up the street, but came to a sudden

halt when the Double Bar hands started to file out from the batwings of the saloon, led by Boyer, Lincoln and Flannigan.

The cowpunchers said nothing: allowed the tacit threat of the levelled revolvers in their fists to convey their intent. There were two dozen of them.

Foster halted as the scowling Texans advanced on him in a line spread out across the street, the anxious Newville citizens shuffling slowly in their wake.

'Don't try to bluff your way outta this, lawman!' the squint-eyed Floyd Boyer snarled. 'You and that murderin' dude was in it together! Everyone in the saloon seen you and him with your heads together before the trouble started!'

There was a buzz of talk among the people of the town: those who had been present in the Trail's End confirming to their fellow citizens that Boyer was telling it like it had been.

'Yeah!' Frank Lincoln added harshly. 'And you're gonna hang for shootin' down Charlie Brewster, Foster!'

'Or we'll drop you where you stand!' Pat Flannigan threatened. 'If you don't tell us where the dude is hidin' out.'

The Texans halted twenty feet away from where the impassively silent lawman stood.

'He ain't armed,' one of the cowpunchers muttered nervously.

'Bill Foster never goes armed,' a townsman said, and was shushed into silence by an anxious woman.

'Neither was Charlie Brewster!' Boyer countered.

'Brewster ain't dead yet,' a Double Bar hand reminded.

'All but, he is,' Lincoln argued.

Foster spoke at last. He raked his gaze along the line of men with levelled guns, then glared fixedly at the three in the centre, said: 'These men are making fools of you others. They and Wayne Ritchie——'

A voice cut in: 'The sheriff's right, boys!'

Only Bill Foster and Adam Steele did not need to turn to look toward the trail boss of the Double Bar. Who had emerged from the centre of the crowd of Newville citizens, stood in unsteady isolation as the people divided into two, backed off to either side of the street.

'All but dead hell!' one of the Texans growled with admiration in his tone as everyone watched Brewster, the front of his shirt slick with blood, stagger forward.

Nobody saw Adam Steele move up alongside Foster, rifle held in a double-handed grip across the base of his belly, thumb on the hammer.

Brewster took a half dozen steps, lurching from side to side. His strength failing fast and near to collapse. In the surrounding silence his rasping voice could be clearly heard.

'It was Ritchie plugged me, you men. Him and his buddies...'

He jolted to a halt, swayed, gasped, pitched forward.

'No!'

Flannigan shrieked the denial as he, Boyer and Lincoln became the focus of accusing stares directed at them by their fellow Double Bar hands.

'Brewster got it wrong!' Lincoln claimed desperately as the other Texans backed away from him and Boyer and Flannigan.

'He was crazy, he was dyin'!' Boyer yelled, waved his gun hand toward Foster and Steele. 'It was them!'

Galloping hoofbeats sounded in the night, the horse racing southward. But nobody paid any attention to the sound as the area at the side of the holding pens became a focal point again. Everybody became aware that the Virginian had joined Foster.

'It was them!'

Boyer bellowed it much louder this time, like he thought the mere volume of his voice would convince his listeners he was telling the truth. Then he swung and steadied his gun hand.

Lincoln and Flannigan instinctively followed his cue.

'Don't!' Foster roared. Then he snarled in anger and shock as Steele crashed into his side, sent him sprawling to the street.

An instant after the Virginian charged down the sheriff, he levelled the Colt Hartford from his hip, squeezed the trigger.

The squint-eyed Boyer took the bullet in his chest, was knocked flat on his back by its fatal impact as his unfired Colt arced away from a flailing hand.

Lincoln and Boyer fired their Colts in unison, but the bullets cracked through the air above the sprawling form of Foster, the diving Steele.

A moment before he hit the ground, Steele triggered the rifle again. The bullet drilled into Flannigan's left side, slammed him into a turn. He was unbalanced, tripped over his own feet, went down with a scream of fear.

Steele was full length on the street, face down. He forced himself into a roll: moved a part of a second before another shot from Lincoln's Colt bit into the hard-packed dirt where he had been sprawled.

Foster struggled to his feet and powered from a crouch toward Lincoln: who cocked his revolver and instinctively tracked it toward the new threat.

The Virginian completed his roll, thumbed back the rifle hammer, exploded a third shot and grinned when he saw a hole appear in the centre of Lincoln's high forehead. The man's hat flew off and a great gout of blood and tissue blasted from the exit wound in the top of his skull.

Then came an abrupt silence while the gunsmoke drifted and the heavily-moustached Frank Lincoln stood for a stretched second like a wax dummy. Before he thudded to the street between the inert Frank Boyer and the quaking Pat Flannigan.

The pent-up breath of the tense watchers was expelled.

'Ritchie's gone!' Burt Baker shrieked from the saloon entrance. 'He took all the money!'

The steers had been strangely, eerily subdued during the barrage of gunfire: as if the earlier panic caused by the fire had exhausted them. But in the silence brought about by the bartender's revelation, they were stirred up again.

Cowhands raced to the pens to calm them, aware that if just one of the spooked Longhorns smashed through a fence, a stampede was certain to get underway.

Sheriff Bill Foster crouched beside the wounded Pat Flannigan, listening intently to the man's rapidly spoken words.

Nobody in the crowd of Newville citizens knew what to do. Then could only watch with apprehension as Adam Steele whirled and sprinted to the railroad depot. Where he ran out to the far end of the platform: to a point from which he could see the distant rider on the south trail.

The horse was being walked now, the rider conserving the animal's strength for a long journey.

Steele dropped on to one knee, raised the Colt Hartford to his shoulder and took careful aim. Squeezed the trigger, vented a low grunt of satisfaction when he saw Wayne Ritchie topple off his mount.

The crowd of local people dispersed to go home.

The Texans bedded down in the undamaged bunkhouse.

When Flannigan was locked in the jailhouse and the dead were being attended to by the Newville mortician, Sheriff Foster rode out to bring back the body of Wayne Ritchie and recover the horse stolen from the stable behind the Trail's End saloon.

After he delivered the final corpse to the mortician and returned the stolen horse, the lawman rode out to the railroad depot. Where he found Adam Steele seated on a bench on the platform, gear beside him.

'Can see why you tote a rifle instead of packing a revolver, stranger,' Foster said as he swung down from his saddle. 'That was quite some long shot.'

The Virginian answered evenly: 'I like to think everybody has something they do well.'

'We were right about there being more to it.' Foster trailed a hand over one of his saddlebags, bulged by what it contained.

Steele nodded, said: 'Ritchie tried to double cross his buddies?'

'Right. It was chickenfeed they took from the stores and the saloon. Flannigan told me they weren't really going to steal it anyway. And I think he honestly believed that.' He patted the saddlebag this time. 'Ritchie was running with thirty-five thousand dollars.'

'The money Brewster was paid for the herd?'

'Right. Charlie Brewster maybe figured there was something queer about the fire and checked wherever he kept the money. He could even have figured it *was* you and me took it when he went to the saloon: seeing as how neither one of us was at the fire.'

'Reckon it doesn't matter what he thought, feller.'

Foster shrugged. 'Guess not, now the poor guy's dead.'

The clock on the courthouse tower struck midnight. The lawman waited until the final note sounded before he said:

'It's another twelve hours until train time, Steele.'

The Virginian nodded, answered: 'And I like riding trains about as much as I like walking, Sheriff.'

Foster did a double-take at Steele, saw he was eyeing his

horse covetously. And suddenly the Newville sheriff extended the reins of the black stallion toward the man seated on the depot bench.

'Here, it'll solve a problem for me, stranger.'

'A problem?' Steele countered as he rose from the bench and Foster began to unsaddle his horse that was not unlike the animal the Virginian had needed to put down out to the west of Newville.

'You saved my life and no mistake,' Foster explained. 'Was wondering what I could do to even up the score on that. A horse seems a cheap price to pay, but——'

'I'll take it in the spirit it's given, Sheriff,' Steele cut in on the lawman as his face developed a pained expression of embarrassment. 'Way I look at it, I paid that bunch of Texans back for what they tried to do to me. But I'm happy to have you see it another way. So nobody owes nobody else any favours, uh?'

Foster shrugged.

Steele started to resaddle the stallion as soon as the other man finished taking his gear off the horse.

'So you're leaving right away?'

'No reason to stay now I have what's necessary to leave.'

Foster shrugged again. 'Suit yourself. But I'd have thought you'd wait until morning. Rest up at the Trail's End.'

Steele said nothing until after he had swung up into the saddle. Then he touched the brim of his Stetson, replied without knowing how prophetic was the response: 'Guess I'm looking for a trail's end, feller, but it's not the one in Newville.'

4

Adam Steele kept his mind active with academic mental exercises while he waited to see if others were going to take a hand in his never-clear-cut plan to recover the stolen Colt Hartford rifle.

He did his waiting on the crest of the southern flank of the rocky valley in which the road agents were resting up, in what seemed to be some kind of derelict former army post. A mile from the head of the valley where ten Indian braves were camped.

His lookout position, picked from his previous vantage point above the Indian's camp, was an isolated stand of pines a quarter of a mile from the stone building surrounded by a partly sound, partly fallen-down wooden fence. Maybe a hundred feet above it. So he had a commanding view of the building with the three horses hobbled outside. And he could also see the more distant Indian camp where not a trace of smoke rose from the fire ashes now.

He had chosen to move to the patch of close-growing trees because of the cover provided by the pines. And when he reached the timber after making a wide swing to the south, he used this cover. He did not go too often to the fringe of the pines, nor did he spend too long at the spot where he could look down on the place occupied by the whites, glance left and lengthen the focus of his eyes to check the Indians were still where he last saw them.

Between times, he paced back and forth or walked around in circles among the trees, his footfalls silent on the thick layer of pine needles. This constant movement served the dual purpose of helping to keep the cold out of his bones and preventing him from submitting to the temptation of sleep. Although since he came within sight of his objective, he was less affected by the cold of the night and neither did he feel so weary.

It was spontaneous thoughts about why this should be so that triggered his mind into a period of constant activity for no specific purpose.

He reasoned that previously he could not be certain that he was going to catch up with the bunch he was tracking, or that he would ever get back the highly prized Colt Hartford. That had been a depressing state of mind to be in, and because of it his thoughts had been of a defeatist nature.

He had to consciously struggle against the conviction that he was too exhausted to go on, for he knew that if he lay down to sleep there was a strong chance he would die of exposure. His life wastefully lost in the foolish pursuit of something that had little intrinsic value. After he had put his life on the line so often when there was so much more at stake it would be crazy to die of the cold on this mountain without ever getting close to what he sought.

Now the situation was entirely different. His objective was virtually in view, so the way he looked at his circumstances had changed.

He felt confident that he would achieve what he had set out to do when he rode away from the stage and his fellow passengers down on the trail. And this confidence strengthened his flagging resolve, warmed him and made the need for sleep less pressing.

This thought through, his restless mind sought fresh subjects to reflect upon. And so as he paced back and forth or moved around in circles under the sometimes doleful, sometimes almost scornful eye of the horse, he found himself examining the other aspects of the situation.

It was probably all academic, he realised. But if he considered all the possible reasons why the whites were in the building and the Indians were camped a mile away, it was likely he would happen upon the right ones. Which could serve a useful purpose—not cause him to be surprised by the totally unexpected—when it came to be time for him to do more than wait and watch.

Just why had the Cowley women and their trio of male companions come up to this valley? Were they working to a preconceived plan that took account of the shelter they knew they would find in the abandoned army post? Or had they stumbled on it by a stroke of good fortune, their spirits soaring as they saw unexpected shelter from the cold of the night? And whether the post had figured in their plans from the outset or not, what did they intend to do come morning?

And what about the braves? Or were they all braves? There could be some squaws asleep under the blankets. All eight of the sleeping Indians could be women, even. But whatever the mix of sex, what were they doing here in these mountains tonight?

As far as Steele was aware, no Indians were indigenous to this area of California. So they were a travelling group. Moving through the mountains without horses, he was certain. For no group, of any race, would risk sleeping far from their mounts in such isolated country as this.

To what nation did the Indians belong? Were they peacefully inclined, or did they carry a grudge against whites?

Had they or the road agents reached the valley first? What were they waiting for? Morning, maybe: so that they could advance on the post openly. Instead of in the night when the peaceful intention of their approach would likely be misinterpreted?

There were whites who, for good reason or bad, would shoot first and ask questions later where Indians were concerned. Especially a superior number of Indians, seen unexpectedly in the dead of night.

Alternatively, if the Indians did not have peaceful intentions, they maybe figured that a daylight approach would get them closer to the enemy before they showed their aggression.

Having gone as far as this along the line of supposition, he next allied the conclusions he had reached with the facts he knew for certain: and attempted to make an educated guess at what the outcome would be if he were not here.

He came up with the logical assumption that the Indians knew there were whites in the building down in the valley. And they intended to make an approach to them. Whether this was going to be by the light of a new day or earlier remained to be seen. It could be they were waiting for the whites to come out into the open, leave the protection of the stout stone walls.

Whichever, it did not auger well for a peaceful outcome: the Indians meant nothing good for the whites.

He was prepared to admit his thinking was biased. For he had been involved in more than his fair share of dealing with Indians before he settled in the Providence River Valley: and he could not recall any occasion when anything but bad resulted. But he was always ready to learn from experience, have his opinions changed on any subject. So on this occasion . . .

He had gone again to the fringe of the timber. For maybe the tenth time in what he estimated to be about three hours. To once more survey the length of the valley between the cliff at its western head and the no-longer-desolate building. It was still brightly lit and deeply shadowed by the glittering moon, and it was easy to see that not everything was as it had been before.

Some of the shadows were moving against the bright backdrop of the rocky ground. The Indians—all ten of them he was careful to count—had left their camp at the base of the cliff. Were slowly but deliberately moving along the valley floor toward the building with the three horses hobbled outside. These horses as immobile as the stone walls and the standing and fallen fences, the animals plainly sensing something different.

The Indians had covered more than half the mile distance between their starting point and the building that was clearly their objective. Were close enough to where Steele stood for him to see they were all braves. Attired in a mixture of clothing that ranged from breechclouts, aprons, leggings and waistcoats of buckskin and homespun Indian origin to tailormade jackets and hats: including some with buttons that gleamed to suggest that the garments were army issue.

All of them carried a pouch, slackly filled with the personal belongings that had been piled in a heap at the camp. Some of them had draped blankets over their shoulders, cape fashion. Four held rifles, levelled in two-handed grips at their hips. Two had revolvers thrust out in front of them.

They advanced in a straggled line, no brave more than six feet from the side of his neighbour, maybe a dozen feet between the Indian at the front and the backmarker. Although the line of advance was crooked, no brave wavered from the straight path, as Steele had done when he zig-zagged from tree to tree after he saw the smoke of their fire, caught a snatch of talk between the two sentries.

So they were as confident about what they were doing as Steele had become when he was certain he was going to get back his rifle. Were arrogantly sure at this early hour of the morning that their approach was unseen by the occupants of the building behind the fence.

The whites were sleeping peacefully at this hour of the dark night, when, it was said, the human spirit is at its lowest ebb: even the healthiest people are closest to death.

It was certainly not a good time to be shocked out of deep, untroubled sleep. A man required long moments to adjust from the subconscious realm of dreams to harsh reality.

So the Indians had timed their move well. If all went according to their plan, two women and three men were indeed close to death in the small hours of this cold morning. They could even die in their sleep.

The two sections of stockade fence that had fallen down were on the south and the east of the building. The braves were moving in from the west, so the fence that still stood on that side of the old army post screened their advance. And they felt no compulsion to veer to the left or right, toward areas of scant cover in the event that a hail of gunfire was exploded toward them.

They knew, without knowing how they could be so sure, that they were not being watched from behind the fence: had no reason to consider there might be an observer positioned elsewhere.

Steele was almost painfully aware of being without his rifle: his fingers stiff from not being able to wrap around the familiar rosewood and metal in a circumstance like this.

The three horses between the fence and the stone wall of the building were no longer immobile. If they continued to sense the proximity of strangers, or now could hear the quiet setting down of moccasinned or booted feet, it no longer caused them uneasiness.

Which did not surprise Steele the horsebreeder. Horses were intelligent to an extent, and they certainly possessed something akin to a sixth sense. But the equine brain required solid evidence of danger to react beyond a pricking of the ears, a freezing into a statue-like attitude for a moment or two.

Steele felt suddenly helpless: more so with each cautious pace the Indian braves took to close with the fence and the building that stood, dark and silent, fifty feet in back of it. His mind raced to try to discover why this should be.

Surely he should have been in the grip of such a sensation of helplessness when he began to lose hope of ever catching up with the people who stole his rifle. Or before that, even: when he had set out riding a horse bare-back and armed only with a knife on the trail of five road agents who were much better equipped. Packing guns he knew they were prepared to use.

But back then he had not allowed himself to consider failure. At first because his resolve was so strong. Then, later, when the cold of the mountain night and the physical demands on his body for rest had combined to become a danger to his survival, it had been unthinkable to consider any kind of negative attitude.

In the present circumstances, it was different: and it took him perhaps a half minute to conclude why this was so.

He did not feel helpless about getting what he wanted. It was just that he could not do anything about what was happening in the moonlit valley below him.

He could only wait and watch as the ten Indian braves advanced inexorably on a group of unsuspecting whites they outnumbered two to one.

But why the hell should he want to help them, damnit!

It was difficult to confine the cursing to his mind: not to snarl a string of obscenities into the silent night as he accused himself of going soft in the head since he changed his way of life.

The people down there in the old army post were not his neighbours in the Providence River Valley. Nor even total strangers.

They were his enemies who had stolen his most precious possession: would have killed him as they had shot down the driver and guard on the stage if he had made a wrong move.

He had no reason to harbour any fellow feeling for them. If the Indians slaughtered all of them and rode off, that would be just fine. Providing they left the Colt Hartford with the engraved plate on the stock behind!

But he thought along this line for just a few moments. Then did curse aloud, softly. And shook his head as if he needed to physically dislodge such a stupid notion.

Was it likely the Indians would leave anything behind except corpses? They were an ill-dressed, badly-equipped band of pony-less Indians, far from their homeland. In process of launching a raid to steal whatever was of use to them. Horses, food, clothing, money and weapons.

Whether or not as a white man he felt any affinity with the bunch of road agents about to be slaughtered by redskins was beside the important point.

Getting his rifle back from ten Indians was surely going to be harder than from five whites: two of them women!

This conclusion reached, it then took only a moment for him to acknowledge that he was not a totally helpless observer.

He had been hunkered down since he first saw the shadow-like forms moving along the valley bottom land. Now he rose to his full height and placed both gloved hands against his bearded face, curled around his mouth to form a bullhorn. He waited until the Indians were within a hundred yards of the fence, sucked in a deep breath of the cold night air. Filled his lungs and emptied them to power the bellowed warning:

'Indians! Wake up inside! Indians!'

His voice, ringing out as loud as he had ever shouted, carried across the valley, hit the far rocky flank and echoed back a distortion of what he had yelled. Then the echo echoed, the sounds of the words twisting and bending back on themselves for what seemed to be many stretched seconds.

But the effect could not have endured more than a moment or two before the horses between the building and the fence started to snort and struggle to break free of their hobbles, banged into each other and two of them fell. And the gelding hitched among the pines behind Steele reacted to the strident shattering of the silence with a high pitched whinny, then snorted in anger when he could not wrench free from where he was tethered to a tree.

The line of braves had wrenched their heads around to peer up at the stand of pines: were able to identify the point of origin of the warning shout before the echo upon echo confused their hearing.

Now snapped out of the frozen attitudes they had adopted. One swung his rifle to aim at where his gaze was directed. By accident or from fear or anger squeezed the trigger to blast off a

104

shot. Whichever, it would have been a chance in a million if he had hit the man who voiced the raucous warning.

And it was just by a fraction of an inch that the bullet missed Steele: thudded into the trunk of the pine beside which he stood to explode pieces of bark that stung his face and lodged in his beard as he dropped back down on to his haunches.

He resisted the impulse to whirl and lunge back from the fringe of the timber, knew he could not possibly be seen from down in the valley so long as he remained anywhere in the cover of the moon-shadowed trees.

Then the unseen man who had shouted the warning was of secondary importance to the Indians. For shouts, the banging open of a door and the thud of heavy footfalls on hard-packed dirt and rock behind the fence had captured their attention.

And Steele felt a tight grin of satisfaction spread across his face when he saw the figures that lunged out of the building through a doorway on the south side. To run in single file around the corner as more rifle shots and then the whoops of the Indians signalled the direction from which the attack was coming.

There had never been any real doubt that Thelma and Belle Cowley and Daryl, Mel and Ricky were holed up in the old army post. But it sure gave him a warm feeling to have it confirmed: see the three men and two women plunge out into the moonlit night. In various stages of undress. All clutching a rifle or a revolver.

Was one of the weapons the stolen Colt Hartford?

Probably the whites added their frantic voices to those of the war-crying Indians. But there was so much noise down in the valley it was not possible for Steele to differentiate between the two languages or even male and female tones.

The Indians were no longer in their straggled line of direct advance. Some had lunged forward, others back, angled off to one side or the other. To seek and sprawl down behind a piece of cover before a barrage of gunfire exploded from behind the timber fence. A fence in which, by design or by the eroding effect of time and mountain elements, there were gaps through which the whites could aim and fire their weapons.

The gun battle raged for another indefinable period of time: many seconds that perhaps totalled a minute as Indians and whites exchanged fire in **seeming panic**. Or maybe aimed at muzzle flashes or areas of drifting gunsmoke.

Each side was surprised as the other after Steele stole the initiative. Both sides were unprepared for a prolonged gunbattle that thudded bullets ineffectively into solid, unfeeling timber or ground.

Eventually, inevitably, Indians and whites alike became aware that such indiscriminate shooting achieved nothing: just rapidly emptied guns in circumstances where there were few reloads available.

Shouts began to be interspersed in the gunfire. Gunfire became sporadic, then faltered to nothing. Individual voices could be heard against the babble of many, and Steele wondered if it was only in his imagination that the more dominant were those of the two women.

The sense of what was being said did not carry up to where Steele squatted, still grinning his satisfaction at what had happened as he waited for events he had set in motion to run their course. Then, when the meaning of what Thelma Cowley shouted to her daughter and the three men might have become comprehensible to him, she realised the shooting had been curtailed and there was no longer a need to shout: lowered her voice in the surrounding quiet.

Then nothing was said by the whites or the Indians that was loud enough to reach up to where Steele watched and waited.

The horse in the trees behind him was as calm as those behind the fence.

Just a faint trace of gunsmoke drifted up toward the stand of pines, irritated his nostrils and threatened him with a sneeze. He pinched his nose with a finger and thumb, covered his beard encircled mouth in case he could not stop the sneeze: vividly recalled how the shout had rang out so loudly, echoed for so long across the rocky valley.

He beat the compulsion to sneeze. Found he was holding his breath in the silence. Then he sensed every eye in the valley was directed up toward the stand of pines where he waited. But he immediately knew this was a false impression.

Maybe some Indians, during this respite in the shooting, glowered malevolently up at the trees, for they knew the warning had been voiced from here. But the shocked-awake

106

whites could have no idea where their rescuer was hidden.

'White Eyes!' an Indian bellowed.

A gunshot exploded from behind the fence. The bullet ricochetted off a rock where somebody thought the voice had come from.

Somebody, a woman, behind the fence spoke harsh-toned words. It would be Thelma Cowley, Steele guessed. Then, after some stretched seconds when nothing of what was said reached him, it was certainly the fat women who bellowed:

'Speak your piece, Injun!'

The answer came at once: 'We have no fight with you!'

The Indians' spokesman had been at about the centre of the line of advance as far as Steele could tell at a distance. For his voice came from behind a boulder that was midway along the line before his warning sent the braves scattering into cover.

'That was friggin' corn you was poppin' just now?' one of the white men yelled, a residue of fear fuelling the fires of his anger.

Once more Thelma's rasping voice was just audible, but what she said was not intended to carry beyond the ears of the group she was censuring, and it did not.

Then the Indian spoke again, loud enough to reach much of the valley. 'We are braves of the Shoshone nation, White Eyes! Just enough to be counted on two hands! We have no fight with you! We travel many days and nights to return to our reservation across the mountains! We seek shelter from the cold in lodge where pony soldiers once——'

'Well, we got here first!' Belle Cowley cut in on him. 'And we ain't sharin'!'

'Unless maybe you got some fine-lookin', firm-feelin' squaw women with you, Injuns!' It sounded like the dark-skinned, leanly-built Mel. He laughed shrilly, maybe trying to underpin fragile courage.

Once again the rasping tone of the older woman conveyed to the Virginian that she was berating one of her companions for speaking out of turn.

'We have nothing to trade!' the Shoshone spokesman countered. And even over such a distance, Steele thought he detected underlying anger at the suggestion of trading a squaw for a night's shelter. 'We have lost everything on our travel. Stolen by White Eyes!'

'Well, we're fresh out of sympathy for heathen savages!' Thelma yelled. 'So you better just move on out of here and find your own place to rest up!'

'You let us do this, White Eyes?'

'What?'

'You let us leave this valley? Not try to kill us?'

There was a pause while Thelma Cowley consulted with the others. Or listened to something somebody else insisted on saying. Then she answered:

'Sure, Injun! You don't start throwin' lead at us like before, we ain't about to mix it with you! We don't want no trouble, neither!'

'How we know you speak truth?'

'What you sayin', Injun?'

'How we know to trust you keep your word, White Eyes?'

Thelma Cowley sounded insulted when she countered shrilly: 'Same away we trust you won't try no tricks, Injun! We don't! You don't! But if nobody trusts nobody else, we're gonna be stuck here like this the rest of the night! We ain't about to do that! Rather fight it out here and now! So you people get the hell outta here! Or get ready to be blasted into the Happy Hunting Ground!'

She sounded too over-confident, like she was having to work at creating an impression to mask her true feelings.

'You wait!'

'Not for friggin' long we won't!' Daryl yelled, and he sounded genuinely ill-tempered: spoiling for a fight.

Just a short time elapsed while a babble of talk was exchanged among the Shoshone, the braves needing to raise their voices to make themselves heard over the wide area of ground across which they had found cover. All the talk was of course in the Shoshone tongue. Which, Steele guessed, acted to heighten the tension felt by the whites behind the fence.

One other nerve-wracking factor in an incomprehensible situation that had exploded them out of untroubled sleep.

To the Virginian the talk was just a distant chatter that gradually faded as one after another the braves completed their say: left it to their spokesman to convey the decision to the whites. Unless, maybe, each brave had made it known to the others he agreed to whatever treachery they had been able to contrive in the available time.

Probably if the discussion had lasted no more than ten seconds it would have been too long for the whites. Perhaps as much as a minute had elapsed when Thelma Cowley made her voice heard again, her tone taut with expanded fear.

'All right, quit the jabberin'! You gonna move on out of here or you wanna fight this scrap through to the finish? All for a lousy roof over your head for what's left of the night!'

'We leave in peace, White Eyes! Under the flag of truce, so you will not shoot?'

'You got our word, Injun!' A sense of relief did not quite put a catch in her voice.

'You speak also for your sentry at top of hill, White Eyes?'
'Sentry?'

The single word rapped out by the older Cowley woman was followed by a series of fast, less stridently spoken questions and answers.

Or that is what Steele assumed them to be as the two women and three men dragged from the backs of their minds recollections of the shouted warning. Where the memories had been driven by fear of the unknown, then the terror of an attack by an unknown number of apparently savage Indians in the short-lived but frantic gunbattle. When there had been no time to think about who had roused them from sleep.

And since the talking had gotten under way, the dangerous present and uncertain future had occupied their minds: made even the immediate past of no importance.

Then Thelma Cowley alone, or the whole bunch of them huddled behind the fence, regained enough composure to come to a logical conclusion. Whichever, it was again the ugly fat woman who raised her voice.

'Adam Steele will do what I tell him, Injun! If he knows what's good for him! I guess the old son-of-a-gun knows what I mean!'

Her voice rose and fell, rose again. Which suggested she did not know where he was concealed: turned her head from side to side to direct her voice to both sides of the valley.

Steele grinned as he experienced a degree of admiration for Thelma Cowley: the way she had worked in the cryptic reference to the Colt Hartford with an inscribed plate that showed it had been given to somebody else named Steele. Then the grin lost every trace of humour as he considered the implied threat in what the woman had yelled.

'Why does your sentry not answer you, White Eyes?' the Shoshone spokesman demanded.

'He ain't never been known to have a lot to say for himself, Injun!' Thelma answered. 'Figures he's said enough so we all know he ain't dumb! That the way it is, you old son-of-a-gun?'

Steele murmured through his gritted teeth, the words carrying no further than his beard: 'Right, lady. Forewarned is forearmed.'

The Secret

After he rode out of Sun City at the end of *The Tarnished Star*, Adam Steele next appeared in San Francisco in *Wanted for Murder*. When that book opened he had been staying at the Havelock Hotel for almost two weeks. What follows took place at some time during that period.

The girl, who was dressed in a coat that was too heavy for the humid heat of the San Francisco evening and clutched a worse-for-wear carpetbag, was no older than eighteen.

She was about the same height as Steele and did not have a striking shape. Probably, he thought, she was downright skinny under the thick black coat that looked like a hand-me-down from a much larger woman. Certainly her hands which gripped the underfilled bag were bony, and her pale-skinned face framed by straggled brown hair was lean to the point of gauntness.

But in spite of her less than prepossessing appearance as she stood on the otherwise deserted dock, peering fixedly out over San Francisco Bay toward the Golden Gate and the Pacific Ocean beyond, Steele felt there was something appealing about her.

The closer he got to her, though, as he took his usual early evening stroll along the waterfront, trying to catch a cooling breeze off the bay and work up an appetite for supper, the more reassuringly convinced he became that there was nothing carnal about his feelings toward the girl.

Hell, there were plenty of readily available women back at the Havelock Hotel on the Embarcadero: if he should tire of the diversion he enjoyed from the games of chance which, with Madam Mary's whores, made the establishment such a magnet for men like the Virginian.

Men with time on their hands and money in their pockets.

Not necessarily a whole lot of money, for the Havelock was far from being the most palatial and therefore the most expensive place where a man passing through the boom town of San Francisco could bed down and have no need to venture out to avail himself of many pleasures of the flesh.

But it served the purpose of Steele, who had been used to the best of everything during his formative years, the span of a continent away. Then been forced by circumstances to endure some of the worst, and had learned to accept whatever came his way and not consider himself too good for what was available at the price he could afford to pay.

As a former Virginian gentleman, though, he did strive to keep up appearances: especially with regard to his dudish style of dress and his gentlemanly manner toward members of the opposite sex, be they young or old, whore or lady.

So, as he moved close enough for his footfalls to be heard by the girl, and she turned with a start to look toward him, he made to raise his left hand to touch the brim of his hat. His right hand remained lightly fisted around the frame of the Colt Hartford rifle, the barrel of which was sloped to his shoulder.

He accompanied the tipping of his Stetson with a quiet smile as far removed from a leer as it was possible to get. In that moment hit upon the notion that she appealed to him as a little girl lost. And he was so taken with her because of the contrast with his own feeling of well-being and self-assurance this evening.

Then she uttered a small sound, kept it from getting any larger by wrenching one of her hands off the handles of the carpetbag, clamping it over her mouth. But the deep-set eyes in her prominently-boned face had enlarged to signal it would have been a scream of fear if she had not trapped the sound in her throat.

She whirled away from him and the bay, dropped her hand to grip the bag again.

'Young lady, you don't need to——' Steele started to assure her, the smile gone in an instant from his face.

He broke off when she froze after taking a single step of what had been intended as a lunge away from him. This time she did not clamp her a hand to her mouth and a shrill shriek burst from her lips. Not loud, but with a quality that communicated a degree of depthless terror that a full-throated scream could not have achieved.

She remained immobile for stretched seconds, her head turned to the side. Then Steele saw what had caused the abrupt halt. For two men had stepped into sight from behind a stack of old and broken wooden crates out front of a warehouse at the rear of the dock.

Young men, one wearing a threadbare suit and the other coveralls over a check shirt, who advanced out of the late afternoon shadows into the failing light of the rapidly setting sun. The suited man a head taller and maybe twenty pounds lighter than the other one, who had red hair and freckles.

Not men, Steele corrected his first impression. A couple of boys, no older than the girl they had frightened so badly. But there was nothing affecting about their attitudes of sneering arrogance as the rangy, better-looking one demanded:

'All right, Suzie: hand it over right now!'

He did not shift his gaze away from the girl. But the fat, freckled youngster was not so singleminded. He merely glanced at her before his attention was drawn to Adam Steele. In an instant was squeezed dry of his fragile self-confidence as he was struck dumb by the sight of the dudishly attired, less than powerfully-built man with a rifle sloped to his shoulder. Flapped his thick-lipped mouth open and closed a few times, at length managed to blurt:

'Collis! Oh shit, Collis!'

He jerked a knife out from a deep pocket of the denim coveralls, with his other hand tugged on the jacket sleeve of his partner: like he could not be certain he had spoken the warning loud enough to draw his attention.

Collis swept his cold-eyed gaze toward the Virginian, was disconcerted for a second or so, then ordered: 'Get the hell away from here, dude! This here is private business between us and her. You tell him that, Suzie!'

Now he drew a knife from under his coat, brandished it with more aggression than his partner who seemed to be as terrified as the girl.

She could now at least turn her head to peer at Steele again. This time her eyes, big as ever, expressed a degree of pleading through the fear as she managed to force out of her constricted

113

throat: 'Collis is right, mister. This is private business. Don't concern yourself with it, please. Just turn around and leave? I don't want anyone else should get hurt!'

'And nobody else will, right JW?' Collis asked, his confidence grown even more now he had Suzie's agreement to his insistence Steele should leave.

'I sure as hell hope not, Collis,' JW answered, but didn't sound hopeful as he continued to stare fixedly at the Virginian.

Collis also eyed Steele, something akin to a half smile twisting his thin lips. Until the rifle was slowly tipped down from the Virginian's shoulder, his left hand came up and across to fist around the barrel as the thumb of the right pressed more firmly on the hammer, but did not click it back.

Collis blinked then. And gulped: looked like whatever he had forced himself to swallow left an evil taste in his mouth.

'Anybody threatens me, it's my business, fellers,' Steele said evenly, aimed the rifle from his hip at the gap between the two of them. The range was about fifty feet, but he started to narrow this as he went on: 'Not that a couple of toothpicks like those knives are much of a threat at this distance. But the closer I get to you, the more they will be, seems to me. You should know, I don't have any worries about anybody getting hurt, long as its not the young lady or me.'

'Oh, shit!' JW rasped.

'Young lady?' Collis blurted with deep contempt. 'Why, she ain't——'

'Oh, my!' JW said in a strangled tone.

'Look, it's not supposed to be——' Collis started.

They brandished the knives with disparate degrees of scowling belligerence. Collis even looked like he was prepared to stand his ground, go down with a bullet in his flesh if the alternative was to back off. While JW looked like it would only require Steele to pull a face and vent a frightening sound to have him whirl and race away screaming.

But Steele had time to just thumb back the hammer of the Colt Hartford as Collis took a step toward him, calling the bluff of the older man.

The Virginian drew a bead on the kid in the threadbare suit.

A gunshot exploded.

Collis hurled away the knife and jerked into a half turn,

brought the hand that had held the knife up and across the clasp at his left shoulder. Then he screamed and staggered out of sight behind the pile of dilapidated packing cases.

Steele was aware that JW had become rigid with shock at the gunshot and its effect, and he switched his gaze to Suzie.

She had one hand plunged inside the carpetbag now. Smoke was wisping out of a blackened hole in the side near the bottom and there was a strong smell of burning from where the muzzle flash of the bullet leaving a gun barrel had seared the thick fabric.

'Oh, my, oh, shit!' JW groaned and hurled down his knife, thrust both hands high in the air, backed off two steps and halted.

'I'm hit, damnit!' Collis yelled. 'Help me, JW! Before I bleed to death.'

'Don't shoot no more, please!' JW pleaded, tears trickling down his freckled cheeks as he snapped his head from side to side to share his beseeching look between Steele and the girl.

'Help me get to a doctor, damnit!' his partner yelled shrilly.

Steele inclined his head, started to bring the rifle barrel up to his shoulder again.

Suzie moved her hand in the bag, enough to push the barrel of a revolver through the bullet hole as she croaked out of her throat squeezed by the enormity of shock at just shooting a man: 'Go help Collis, JW. And you two just better not ever try to get it again, okay?'

'Suzie, I——'

'Just go, JW!' she implored, and now she sounded weary.

'Yeah, sure! That's what we'll do. We'll leave. Gee, I'm real sorry to——'

He turned, dropped his arms to his sides and went from sight behind the old crates. Did not break off the babbling until Collis snarled something at him that sounded like it included a great deal of obscenity.

Steele was unconcerned that the more belligerent kid might be planning to get even there and then. For the girl maintained a scowling watch on the area where she aimed the gun in the carpetbag. Then, after he had looked along the dock in both directions, not been surprised to realise something so mundane as a gunshot had failed to create interest on the city's waterfront, he returned his attention to Suzie. Saw how the tension had drained out of her attitude as the expression on her profile altered from fear mixed with hatred to deeply felt relief.

'Oh, God,' she gasped at length, and snapped her head around to look at him. 'That was awful. I ain't ever shot anybody before.'

Steele advanced slowly on her, his unblinking gaze directed at an ever broadening view of the area beyond the stack of crates. When he stood beside her, he could see the entire length of an alleyway between two double storey warehouses. It was empty along its hundred feet length and twenty feet width, with no shadowed doorways or windows in the flanking walls. The roofs of the warehouses were beyond the reach of an able-bodied man, let alone one with a bullet in him.

'They've gone,' Suzie said dully. 'Out at the other end of the alley.'

'How long have you carried a gun, young lady?' Steele asked as he looked at her again, saw she was gripping the carpetbag with both hands once more holding it like much depended upon what it contained. Which had to be more than a pistol.

'Just since this morning.'

'So you learned a lesson faster than a lot of people do, Miss . . .?'

'Kimball. My name's Susan Kimball. Mostly I just get called Suzie.'

This close to her, as she suffered the after effects of shock but was no longer gripped by terror, he thought she was no older than fifteen. Which accounted for the underdeveloped skinniness of her body. But did not match the maturity in her deep-set, dark-coloured eyes that he was sure had seen more than most girls of her age. Certainly not many fifteen year olds had witnessed the result of blasting a bullet into the flesh of a fellow human being.

'Okay, Suzie Kimball, so you learned early that if you carry a gun, chances are you'll find a reason to use it.'

She shrugged her narrow shoulders. 'It just seemed like a good idea to fire it, mister. I could've missed both of them or killed either of them. I'm really grateful you were around. Way I only winged Collis Little, they could've——'

Steele cut in: 'Could have doesn't count in the real world,

116

Miss Kimball.'

She pouted as she reminded: 'Most everybody calls me Suzie. I told you that.'

'We'll probably never see each other again,' he pointed out as he again revised his estimate of her age. Thought maybe she was seventeen, or even eighteen. Certainly the pout looked too young for her gaunt face.

'You want to sleep with me?' she asked baldly.

'What?' Even though he had decided she was a young woman of the world rather than a little girl lost, the single syllable came out hard.

And, like it had a physical force, she stepped back a pace from him, did a double-take at his expression then shrugged and explained: 'To pay you back for helpin' me outta the jam with Collis and J.W. Baldry, mister. Mister who, anyway? In case this ain't the end of it, what should I call you?'

'Name's Steele. Adam Steele. No offence intended Suzie Kimball, but you're not the kind of female I'd choose to take to bed. And in this town a man has a wide choice.'

She shrugged again, and turned toward the direction he had been heading when he saw her standing on the dock.

He was ready to let that be the end of it. Tried to tell himself as he waited there for her to leave that he hoped it was the end of it. But she paused, looked back at him, gestured he should go with her. And behind an impassive mask he told himself he was a fool as he went to join her, rifle sloped to his shoulder.

She walked with the bag held in a two-handed grip in front of her, her knees banging against it.

'I ain't offended, Mr Steele,' she told him. 'Like Collis said, I ain't no lady, not by any manner of means. And I can tell you that you don't have to tell me what kinda company a man can buy in this San Francisco. I been sellin' what every girl's got to sell in a place on Pacific Street for most of a year now.'

Steele directed a sidelong glance at her as she made the admission in an unconcerned monotone. And he was sure she was not setting out to shock him, either with the truth or a pack of sordid lies. And, as when the gunshot had not drawn any responses from the craft moored along the waterfront and the buildings behind, he was not surprised that a girl of seventeen or fifteen—even younger than that, maybe—sold herself in this

117

town.

'Now you have something else to sell?'

'What?'

He looked longer at her. Saw her face muscles stiffen, her arms become rigid as her bony hands clutched the carpetbag more tightly than ever.

She sensed his curious gaze and sent a fast sidelong glance at him. Then peered straight ahead, into the gathering darkness of a night that would have been black under a thickly clouded sky were it not for lamplit windows of the city and portholes of the moored ships.

'I'm not sure how far I can trust you, Mr Steele,' she said anxiously.

'Every man has his price,' he answered. 'But right now I reckon I've got everything I want. Unless you count I'm short a million or so dollars.'

She looked at him sharply this time. Was relieved to see his grin and tried one of her own. She needed to experiment with it for a while, at length found an expression that felt comfortable: and maybe by coincidence it drained some of the gauntness out of her features, made her look almost pretty.

Steele was still pleased to know he did not feel sexually attracted to this little girl who almost certainly had entertained many more men than he had taken women.

'You stayin' here in 'Frisco, Mr Steele?' she asked suddenly. Not smiling, her decision made. Eager to implement it.

'Place called the Havelock Hotel on the Embarcadero. I hear it's not so wild as some of the places along the Barbary Coast where you're in business.'

She could not be tempted into a smile again. Instead she scowled in response to his grin, shook her head violently as she corrected:

'I worked there in somebody else's business. I don't do that kind of work anymore.'

The Virginian felt his own anger rise to the same level as that of Suzie Kimball because he suddenly resented her attitude. But he decided to give her another chance.

'I'm happy for you,' was all he said, not sounding happy.

'Could we go to your room?' she asked flatly.

'No.'

'Oh?'

'If I took you to my room, you'd be considered competition for the bunch of whores who work at the Havelock and maybe I'd get tossed out for bringing you there.'

She stopped abruptly, and he was certain that if she said anything that implied a recrimination this time, he would give up on her. For it would not be too difficult to suppress the curiosity he felt about Suzie Kimball, pistol-packing ex-whore.

But it was not what he had said that caused her to stop there. They were at the mouth of another alley between two large warehouses, one of which smelled strongly enough of spices to mask the more pungent, less pleasant waterfront aromas. She looked like she was unsure if she should turn into the alley.

Then, just as she was about to say something to Steele, both had their attention drawn to where a three-masted schooner was berthed alongside the dock opposite the warehouse that did not smell of spice.

Footfalls had begun to sound on the decking, then a line of five men started down the gangplank, calling out cheerfully to each other in a foreign language. As soon as they stepped on to dry land they noticed the couple at the mouth of the alley and gathered into a huddle.

There was much laughter in with the talk now, and much jabbing of each other with elbows. Then one of the seamen was elected spokesman and he left the group to approach the Virginian and the girl.

He was freshly washed up and shaved and his teeth gleamed exceptionally white against the sun and sea burnish of his skin.

'*Scusa señor*?' he greeted, showing more of his teeth in an eager grin which he directed at Steele while his dark eyes kept shifting their appraising gaze to Suzie Kimball.

'Feller?'

Now the foreign seaman waved a hand at the girl, asked: 'You do special low price for *cinque, señor*?'

He held up his hand, splayed to display the four fingers and thumb, turned his head and nodded toward his shipmates. But suddenly he realised something was badly wrong when he saw their smiles fade into frowns.

He turned his head slowly, until forced to halt the move when the side of his jawbone came up against the muzzle of the Colt Hartford: the rifle angled between Steele's hip and the man's head.

'Doing a special on death tonight, feller,' the Virginian told the abruptly terrified man evenly. 'You die fast, and I don't make any charge for the bullet.'

'*Señor*, I make the mistake, I know it!' the seaman blurted.

'Making mistakes helps to make us human.'

'*Si, señor*.' Mounting fear made his voice little more than a whisper.

'There's no more fertile ground for sowing wild oats than this town,' Steele said, and eased the rifle muzzle away from the sweat-sheened flesh of the man. 'Go find yourselves another furrow to plough.'

He made use of the freedom he had to nod. Then sought a wider freedom, backed away. So did his shipmates, their retreat getting faster after he rejoined them.

As they moved along the dock, talk restarted, interspersed with hollow laughter. The scowls and sneers directed back at Steele and Suzie Kimball tacitly conveyed the gist of what they were saying.

'They think I'm like a piece of string without even any knots in it,' the girl translated evenly. 'And they hope to meet up with you when you don't have the rifle, Mr Steele.'

She gestured for them to head into the alley and he followed when she did so, asked:

'You speak Spanish?'

'Yeah, ain't I just a bundle of surprises, Mr Steele? I understand it better than I talk it. Same as with Mexican, French, Russian, and even some Japanese. Whores in a town full of whores have a lot of spare time. I happened to find out I got a gift for learnin' languages. And it used to help some in my job. Which I'm out of now. So thanks for protectin' my honour back there.'

'It was nothing, Susan.'

Their voices echoed between the high walls of the warehouses on either side and they both instinctively lowered them. Steele, as cautious as he always endeavoured to be in alien surroundings, kept careful watch on the far street end of the alley, listened for sounds from the waterfront behind.

'Thanks for that.'

'You really want to thank me, you could maybe tell——'

'I mean thanks for callin' me Susan,' she broke in. 'Last time I can remember that happenin', it was my Dad. He called me Susan just before he died after the Indians hit our wagon. Ma didn't live long enough to say anythin'.'

She made a sound that seemed to be a half sob, half growl of irritation with herself. Shook her head as they emerged from the alley on to a narrow street as deserted as the dock had been before first the two kids with knives and then the Spanish seamen had shown up to make trouble. But it was darker, none of the lights from ships or buildings reaching to it.

'You have some place in mind you want to go?' he asked as she looked about her, like she was trying to get her bearings.

'The railroad depot.'

'Somewhere this way,' he said, and started forward.

She remained where she was, said: 'I've had this town. The fastest way out of it is by train, right?'

He stopped, looked back at her to reply: 'Trains go faster than boats.'

'Uh?'

'You were staring out toward the ocean when I first saw you.'

'Was I? Yeah, I was. I was thinkin', Mr Steele. Tryin' to figure out what I oughta do.' She still sounded indecisive, then confirmed. 'I still ain't sure. Not absolutely sure.'

'Well I am, young lady,' he told her. 'Still have the same plan I started out with. Eat some supper and play some cards, maybe a little roulette if I feel lucky. First, though, I have to finish this walk I already started. Never planned to take in the train station, but if you get the lead out, I reckon I'll——'

'I need to get there without too many people seein' me.'

He turned and walked back to her. And his hard attitude, the

121

way a long sigh burst out through his compressed lips, made her catch her breath, lock rigid from the tips of her fingers curled around the carpetbag handle to the rest of her skinny frame as she backed against the warehouse wall.

'You playing me for a sucker, Miss Kimball?' he asked grimly.

'What? No . . . No, I need you to help me! Please will you help me?'

'You've been a whore in a Pacific Street cathouse for almost a year, you said. I'm a passing-through stranger in this town. So you ought to know better than me how to get to the railroad depot?'

'Yeah, but I'm so scared, mister. I can't think straight. Every time I think about what happened, I——'

'Anyway,' Steele cut in on her rapidly spoken excuses, 'if you want to get there without anyone happening to see you, I'm not so sure I want to go with you. On dark streets at night or with the sun shining on——'

She cut in on him this time, blurted: 'I stole somethin'!'

And she brought up a hand to cover her mouth as she did at the outset. This time it was like she was trying to push back down her throat the words she had spoken.

Steele said evenly: 'I figured that out. You and Little and Baldry is my guess. Unless you stole it from those two boys?'

She wrenched her head one way and then the other. The whites of her eyes showed up as starkly as the teeth of the Spanish seaman while she surveyed the darkened street, terrified that somebody would overhear the exchange.

Steele had not shouted, but neither had he made any effort to keep his voice down. Her voice was a rasping whisper when she begged:

'Please, isn't there someplace we can go? I'll tell you everythin', every last detail. But it's got to be somewhere there's no chance of us being seen or heard. Then it'll be up to you, if you want it to go any further.'

Steele was again mad at her. His hands itched to reach out, take hold of her bony shoulders and shake her. But he was just as mad at himself: because he knew he was not about to submit to the compelling desire to whirl away from her, start to follow the plans he had for the evening and leave this girl to her own devices.

She sensed his tension and uttered a sound that was just a sob, nothing else. And tried to press herself even closer to the wall, like she expected him to hit her.

Then he let the pent up breath rasp out through gritted teeth, said grimly: 'Follow me. Don't ask questions, don't criticise, don't whine, don't do any damn thing except stay close until we get to where we're going.'

He turned from her and strode away. And for what seemed a long time he heard only his own determined footfalls on the street: made a conscious effort not to look back to see if she was still pressed against the warehouse wall, or if she had drifted silently back into the alley to return to the waterfront.

Then he heard her hurrying footsteps. They were coming closer. And although to tried to tell himself this irritated him, he could not ignore the warm glow that spread through him. This damn kid had really gotten to him!

When she caught up with him, matched her pace to his, he glanced at her. Saw she was moving in the same way as on the dock after the run-in with Little and Baldry: the carpetbag gripped in both hands in front of her, her knees banging against it while she gazed fixedly straight ahead. But maybe she held herself even more rigid now as she concentrated on staring into the middle distance. Perhaps afraid if she dared to look at him she would feel compelled to break the rules he had laid down. Which would cause him to run out of the fragile patience she had already tested close to the limit.

This was Steele's sixth day in San Francisco. Most of the time he had remained inside the Havelock Hotel, ventured out only for an early evening stroll which tonight had been disrupted by meeting this frightened young...

Young whore, he settled on. Whether a girl or a woman, she was a self-confessed whore and if he thought of her in those terms it might prevent him being tempted to become more interested in her than in the contents of her bag.

He looked at her again, aware she had started to breath noisily hard. Wondered if she was purposely over-emphasising her weariness, hoping he would get the message and slow his pace without her having to speak, which he had forbidden.

This degree of compliance added to the little girl lost

appearance that had stirred his disconcerted interest in her. And as he saw this, he shifted his gaze hurriedly away from her, devoted his entire attention to finding the destination he had in mind.

This was a small park, an oasis of country surrounded by the city which he had come upon during his first early evening stroll. It was in the commercial area of the city that was deserted after the people who worked in the surrounding office buildings and factories had finished for the day.

Here Steele spent a little time each evening. Sat on a rock on a grassy mound beside a stand of young trees. Where, with a little imagination, he could think himself a long way from San Francisco on warm, balmy nights when no salt breeze came in off the ocean to bring with it the distant hum of the great city.

This was where he took the reluctantly submissive Suzie Kimball. By a route that was unfamiliar to him and took no account of whether the streets were dark and deserted or brightly lit and starting to fill with people out for a night on the town.

While he appeared to be nonchalantly unconcerned with any aspect of their constantly changing surroundings, he maintained his customary careful watch on all sides. Failed to see anybody who showed more than passing interest in the girl and himself.

She remained silent, outside of her noisy rapid breathing. But he was always aware of her changing moods without need to look at her. Knew she was constantly impatient to get to where he was taking her, sometimes was afraid, or angry, or resigned to the inevitable.

She gave a little gasp when Steele abruptly turned off the street, to go between fastened-open wrought iron gates and entered the park. Then she needed to quicken her pace to catch up with him, uttered another gasp that was close to being a small scream when he came to a halt.

'It's all right,' he told her. 'We're here, Susan Kimball. You can take a load off your feet. And a load off your mind.'

She looked around and shivered like she was cold in the warm darkness, asked: 'What is this place, Mr Steele?'

'I don't know what it's called. But to me it's like a piece of home. Which you won't understand, but you don't have to.'

124

He sat down in his usual place, on a smooth-surfaced slab of rock at the base of the knoll beside the trees. The humid air was not stirred by any breeze tonight and no sounds drifted in from the city. It was more than ever like Virginia in mid-summer.

The girl remained standing, looked around her in the same manner as back at the warehouse on the waterfront. Like a wild animal which knows it is the prey of others, testing the surroundings for sight or scent of a predator. But finally she sat on the rock beside Steele, rested the carpetbag on her lap, said in a rasping whisper:

'You were right. I've got somethin' to sell. Or that's what I thought. Now all I want to do is get rid of it. Forget I ever had it.'

'We're through talking around in circles, young lady,' Steele growled. 'Tell it to me plain and simple. Or go find somebody else to listen to you.'

'You'd really leave it like that? Without knowin' what's happened today?'

'It was none of my business at the start. I'm just out for my usual evening walk. Which has been a little more eventful than usual, that's all.'

'You're a strange man, Mr Steele.'

'Yeah, I've lived with me all my life and I still don't understand myself sometimes. You going to tell me what's in the bag?'

'Something that could get you the million bucks you figure you're short of,' she answered tensely. 'If you know how to go about it.'

She held the bag with just one hand, reached into it with the other.

Knowing it was unreasonable, the Virginian nevertheless experienced an icy touch of fear in the warm night. Tightened his grip on the Colt Hartford resting across his thighs as he recalled what happened the last time Susan Kimball reached into the bag.

His night vision seemed to be abruptly intensified, like a glittering full moon had appeared, when she drew out her hand. Wrapped around the barrel of the revolver that had put a bullet into Collis Little. A big Colt, forty-five calibre, with a gleaming plated finish and carved pearl butt plates.

'Here, take it,' she said.

Steele's night vision returned to normal. It always had been, of course. His imagination had played a trick, in this place where on other nights he had come to imagine he was back home.

He raised the rifle an inch off his lap, said: 'I don't have need of another gun.'

'This isn't just a gun, Mr Steele,' she answered. 'It's a special one.'

'Special? It looks like a fancy model of a——'

'I meant it belongs to somebody special. You'll see for yourself if you read what it says along the side of the barrel. Here, take a look and——'

A gunshot exploded. Out in the open it sounded much louder than the one the girl had fired, muffled within the carpetbag.

And suddenly Susan Kimball was not sitting on the slab of rock beside the Virginian any more. The force of impact of the bullet that blasted into her flat chest almost lifted her slight frame into the air before it sprawled her out on her back across the base of the grassy knoll. Instantly dead, the spasms that jerked and twitched her sparsely-fleshed body for long moments were simply her nervous system suffering its death throes.

Steele saw the bullet blast a hole in the girl's chest and snapped his head around to locate where the shot had been fired from. Instinctively he tightened his grip around the barrel and frame of the rifle, his initial feeling of anger at his failure to realise there was danger in the park.

Then he experienced a brand of relief that triggered an icy calm in the wake of the searing rage, a calm which dried the sweat squeezed from his every pore. A grief compounded by utter helplessness when he saw who had fired the shot, knew he could not defend himself if he was next.

He had no chance to avenge the brutal killing of Susan Kimball, so he looked back at her: saw her slight form shudder a final time, then become totally still. The bullet hole and blossoming blood stain hardly showed against the dark fabric of the too heavy coat.

'It doesn't have to happen to you,' a man said evenly.

He was Susan Kimball's killer. A trace of smoke still wisped from the muzzle of his repeater rifle which he needed to swing just a couple of inches to the left to aim at a new target as Steele turned to look at him again, longer and harder now.

Only then did he pump the action, to eject the spent cartridge case and jack a fresh round into the breech. But this rifle was not the only weapon aimed at Steele. There was another repeater and ten revolvers. For a dozen men had come to assassinate the little girl lost whom the Virginian had found so appealing. Men poised to assassinate him if he did not co-operate.

But he would have co-operated with them if they had been far fewer in number. Because he knew the kind of men they were, the kind of job they did, from the badges pinned to coat lapels and shirt or vest fronts.

They were tall and broadly-built, older than thirty but less than forty. With hard-set mouths and coolly-gazing eyes. Looking, at first impression, like they were all members of the same family. Which, in a way, they were.

Lawmen, but the shape of their badges—shields rather than stars—indicated they were a special breed of peace officer. Not often seen in the West: seldom recognised for what they were anywhere.

Steele said: 'I'd rather you just told me to go to hell. Instead of sending me there.' There was a catch in his voice he told himself was caused by grief, rather than the enormity of the situation in which he was caught up.

'She tell you much?' the girl's killer asked. He was one of three men with a moustache. It was a lighter colour than that of the other two and did not curve down at the sides of his mouth. It was all that distinguised him from the other eleven men in the darkness of the park that drew such little light from the surrounding city.

Steele moved a foot to nudge the elegant revolver that had sprung from Susan Kimball's hand as the bullet blasted her young life out of her.

'She didn't get to say anything about anything that would interest Government men.'

'These Government men owe you.'

'What for?'

'Bringing the little whore to a place where this could be done without causing a fuss.'

'I didn't do that,' Steele said as the men with rifles angled them at the ground and those with revolvers pushed them into hip and shoulder holsters.

'I know you didn't realise what you were doing, but you assisted us.'

He confirmed he was the top hand when he issued instructions and two men came to get the girl who looked even skinnier in death. They were careful not to cross between Steele and the men with guns who could bring them back to the aim in a moment.

'Do us another favour? And one for yourself, too?'

'What's that?'

He waved a hand toward one of the men wearing a suit bulged by a shoulder holster, said: 'Don't interfere when this gentleman comes to get that pistol at your feet?'

Steele looked down at the ornate Colt.

The top man warned sharply: 'You won't be doing yourself any favour if you look at it any closer!'

Steele nodded to the man designated to retrieve the revolver, who advanced cautiously. Then, as the temporary undertakers carefully lifted the corpse of the girl, he stooped and took the gun. He left the carpetbag where it lay, took a length of oilskin out of a jacket pocket and wrapped the revolver tightly in it, lodged the package against his side between the elbow and armpit of his right arm.

No words were spoken, nor was there any change in the impassive expressions of all the men. But Steele clearly discerned a sudden easing of high tension.

Then one man vented a low whistle, head turned to direct the signal in a particular direction. Hooves clopped and wheelrims rattled on a street, a few moments later the sounds changed as the rig with two horse in the traces entered the park.

It was a small, dark-coloured, windowless, four-wheeled wagon similar to scores that could be seen on San Francisco's streets, making deliveries.

The man with the revolver climbed up to sit beside the driver as soon as the rig came to a halt. And another man swung open the double doors at the rear.

The corpse of Susan Kimball was placed inside with a degree of reverence, then the rifles were tossed aboard, the doors closed.

A hand banged on a side panel and the rig was steered into a tight turn and started to leave the park.

It seemed like all the Government men were going to move off in its wake: each of them taking off his badge to be stowed out of sight. But one of them held back: the spokesman who was clearly the most senior in the chain of command.

Steele wondered briefly if he could have guessed his line of work now that the man was without the rifle and did not wear a badge. But then he realised this was a futile exercise, asked:

'Will her grave be marked?'

'What?' the Government man asked as he closed the twenty feet gap to half the distance.

'If there's to be a marker on where she's buried, she preferred to be known as Susan Kimball.'

'We know her name.' He sounded impatient. It was the first time his voice had been anything except monotone.

'She was known in this town as Suzie, feller,' Steele said. 'Suzie was a whore. She planned to leave that business.'

'I'll let it be known. Disposal of the corpses will be handled by others.'

'Corpses?'

'Collis Little and John Walter Baldry. At the other end of the alley from where the whore wounded Little.'

Steele nodded, said sardonically: 'A dozen fellers handled that with even less fuss. I didn't hear any shot back there.'

Now a frown of anger came to the man's moustached face as he resented the Virginian's irony. But this display of emotion lasted no longer than the show of impatience earlier. He answered impassively: 'It requires manpower to search a city the size of San Francisco for three individuals, mister. It took us all day to track them to the waterfront. We could have handled the whore just as quietly if there hadn't been an innocent bystander there.'

This time Steele wondered if the man had to make much effort to keep from implying criticism by tone or expression.

'He's a pretty important feller, I guess?'

'Who?'

'The one with his name on the revolver.'

'So she told you that much. Not his name?'

'No.'

'What else?'

'Nothing, unless I take the trouble to read between the lines. And if I do too much of that, I won't be doing myself any favours, uh?'

'You're a whole lot smarter than Suzie ... Susan Kimball was.'

'She was a bright girl. She knew a handful of languages.'

'But not bright enough to steer clear of the likes of Collis Little and J.W. Baldry.'

'She was through with them.'

'We saw that. We thought that maybe she was getting ready to toss the gun into the bay. Before you came along, then Little and Baldry showed up.'

'Would it have made any difference to her if she did that?'

'Maybe we'd have talked to her, even give her some money. Not so much as she and those two cheap crooks hoped to squeeze out of Uncle Sam. But enough for her to give up whoring. Call herself Susan.'

'It's what her parents used to call her before she was orphaned by an Indian attack and got——'

'Spare me her sad story, mister!' the Government man said, sharp-toned again. 'I did what I had to do to keep her from telling you an even sadder one.'

'Like you to tell me, feller.'

'What?'

'I feel myself party responsible for how Susan Kimball died. I want to know why she had to die that way.'

'What was she to you?'

Steele moved the Colt Hartford. He lifted it up off his lap and sloped it to his shoulder, thumb hooked to the hammer. At no time was the rifle aimed at the Government man, but there was a hint of a threat in the move. Enough to have galvanised his partners into action if any had remained behind in the park with him.

The Virginian felt sick to his stomach from the tension, had to pause for a couple of calming seconds before he could answer:

'She was someone who trusted me because I told her she

could. I didn't purposely betray that trust, but I have to know why I'm just sitting here, letting it all happen.'

'If I was a man who caved in when a gun was pointed at me, I wouldn't have the job I do, mister.'

'I realise that, feller,' Steele told him. 'And I also realise that if you've got any family, they'll be real proud of whatever honour Uncle Sam gives you posthumously.'

'Mister, you're being stupid if you figure you can——'

Steele felt confident enough they were alone to tip the rifle down from his shoulder, grasp the barrel in his free had and thumb back the hammer as he aimed it at the Government man. Who stayed angry, but did not show any sign of fear. He simply curtailed what he was saying to watch the Virginian rise to his feet: resigned to the inevitable.

Steele said: 'I'm not a crook, feller. Small or big time. I was on the losing side in the war, but now that's over and done with, I consider myself a patriot. Like the little girl you just shot down, I don't have a family. I do have a little self-respect. She never had a chance to build any for herself.'

'Mister, you——'

'Hear me out, feller, I'm nearly through,' Steele said. 'Patriotic or not, I'll kill you for what you did to that girl. Unless you tell me why she had to die that way. And it'll only add to my self-respect, mister.'

'Without the gun, nothing will stand up.'

'I just want it to stand up for me, feller.'

The Government man thought about it while he toyed with his moustache.

Steele encouraged: 'I don't want you to name names. Just sketch in an outline and I'll fill in the details for my own satisfaction.'

The man finished fingering his moustache, but did some more inactive thinking about the proposition until finally he gave a nod, grunted, spread a grimace across his features and said: 'Figure you've had enough warnings, mister. Just have to hope you believe I'm as serious about them as I'm certain you'd kill me if you took it into your head to do so.'

Steele acknowledged the truth of this with a nod. Then he sloped the Colt Hartford to his shoulder and the Government man began at once.

131

'There are some big names in San Francisco right now. They came for a high level conference with the Mexicans. No announcements were made and the whole thing was top secret. What they've been talking about doesn't concern you. I've told you this much to explain why men such as me are in the city in such numbers.'

'Diplomacy has never been my strong suit, feller,' Steele said in response to the questioning frown.

'Okay. The conference ended yesterday. But our job didn't. It won't until certain gentlemen are safely back in Washington. Which will be as soon as possible now. But last night...'

He shook his head, pulled a face, went on: 'Some important men aren't any different from some lesser mortals when a heavy job of work is done, Steele. They like to have a good time. And if they're far away from their nearest and dearest they're inclined to kick over the traces harder than when they're home. If you understand what I'm saying?'

'Sure. And San Francisco is a town full of traces ready and waiting to get kicked over.'

'Right. We knew it. We expected to have to grease some palms, smooth some rough patches and buy some silence. It goes with the territory. But last night, something got a little out of hand. The place of entertainment we picked out didn't suit the tastes of somebody who'd had a lot too much liquor. It impaired his judgment, and he no longer understood the need for discretion.

'In short, he went missing. And we didn't find out about it until the damage was done. Hell of a thing, mister.'

'I reckon it had to be.'

'The two whores he was with recognised him, which wasn't surprising. There can't be many people in this entire country with an ounce of sense who wouldn't recognise him.

'Naturally, I guess, these ladies thought they could raise the ante in the games they were playing. But our man sobered up then. He knew it wouldn't end there. And the crazy sonofa... Instead of paying up and then having us take care of those whores, he pulled out his gun and he shot both of them in the head. Then he got the hell out of that Barbary Coast cathouse real fast.'

'But he forgot to take his fancy gun with him?'

132

The Government man nodded. 'One of a matched pair with his name engraved on it, along with the engraved signature of the foreign head of state who made him a present of the guns.

'He was running scared, but we were lucky enough to pick him up early. And soon as we heard what happened, we had to start picking up the pieces without involving the local law. The mess had to be kept secret.

'A couple of dead whores were no problem. There aren't many days go by without a serious wounding or a killing in one of the houses and more perpetrators get away with it than are ever apprehended.

'But the gun was missing. So was the cathouse bartender, one Collis Little, J.W. Baldry who pushes broom at the place and the whore who worked in the room next to that where the two women were shot: Suzie Kimball.

'The rest you know or can guess, right mister?'

Steele replied evenly: 'It took you all day to track them down. And if I hadn't shown up on the dock when I did, everyone who knew about this mess outside of Uncle Sam's men would be dead and gone.'

'That's right. We figured we got lucky when we found them all together on the dock. Why they separated we don't know. Maybe they had a falling out or maybe the girl took the gun and ran, they only caught up with her when we did. It doesn't matter, though. We just knew who the men were and we silenced them. Then we stayed close to you and the whore until you brought her here. Where things could be handled as discreetly as on the waterfront.

'And if she hadn't started to show you the gun and tell you what happened, it would have been handled even——'

'Sure,' Steele cut in on him. 'I'm grateful to you.'

'Good. I'm going to turn around and leave now. And if you kill me for killing the whore, then I can promise you my colleagues will find you and you'll end up the same as me and the whore and Little and Baldry. And it won't make a centsworth of difference to the man who is responsible for all of this.

'He's the man who likes his liquor in quantity and his women in great variety. And so there's sure to be other times.'

'What will you tell your partners you stayed behind to talk to me about, feller?' Steele asked.

The Government man shrugged, answered: 'The weather? The state of American-Mexican relations? How sorry I am to have killed a little girl who didn't know what she was getting into—maybe? Fancy guns: including that revolver action sporting rifle with a presentation plate on it you tote around?'

Steele had turned to leave the park by a different route to the Government man. He paused to say: 'Yeah, that could be quite a coincidence.'

'Coincidence?'

'It was my Pa's rifle. The plate tells how he was given it by the president of the United States, Abraham Lincoln.'

'Try not to lose it, mister, that's all I'll say,' the Government man responded just before he went from sight into the trees.

'Right,' Steele murmured as he moved off to complete his evening stroll. 'But it could be a coincidence: you have to grant that.'

5

It had been less than half a minute since the Shoshone brave and Thelma Cowley had finished their exchange about Steele's lack of response.

During that time the Virginian at the fringe of the pines on the crest of the valley's southern side sensed the mistrust of the Indians and the intrigue of the whites. He waited for an outburst of anger from either side if the Shoshone did not move.

But then they did move. Rose from out of their cover in the bottom land of the rocky valley and formed into a single file to start forward. As far as Steele could judge, it was their spokesman who carried a rifle above his head, a strip of light-coloured fabric tied to the barrel: waved it slightly from side to side as he moved out ahead of the others, their weapons held low and pointed at the ground.

They advanced at a measured pace along a path that swung around the southern side of the building, where the fence had collapsed and the whites would be without cover if they remained as they were to watch the Indians.

But the fact that the two Cowley women and the three men had been surprised by the Indian attack and were worried by the presence of a man they were certain was Adam Steele had not addled their brains. They hurriedly unfastened the hobbles on the three horses, led them round to the northern side of the old army post.

As he watched this, along with the shuffling advance of the Shoshone, the Virginian was convinced that this would not be the peaceful end of the incident.

The Indians would not pass on by the stone building partially protected by a timber fence where, at the outset, they could only have expected to rest for the night, sheltering from the mountain cold. Unexpectedly, they had seen an opportunity to improve their lot: with three horses and whatever else the owners of the animals possessed that might be of use to a party of underprivileged, ill-equipped nomadic Indians.

Three riders, to match the number of horses, they must have thought. And the favourable odds of out-numbering the enemy more than three to one had tempted them to try a furtive approach.

But the odds were suddenly shortened when five guns exploded a hail of lead at them. After a sixth white signalled his presence on the hill.

Or maybe the Shoshone did intend to move right on by, Steele allowed. In which case, it would be the whites who were getting ready to open fire on . . .

Steele murmured into his beard: 'Shit.'

For suddenly, no more than another half minute since the Indians started forward and his mind began to consider numbers, he saw he had badly miscalculated the situation below him.

Three horses, three men and two women were hidden on the blind side of the army post, that was for sure.

But there were not ten figures in the line of Shoshone! He had been so intently watching and waiting for the Indians or whites to abuse the flag of truce he had failed to spot one brave was missing.

He abruptly felt much colder than he should be on account of the night air and his inadequate clothing. An icy cold that attacked every part of his body and seemed to literally freeze his backbone, root him rigidly to the spot where he stood. Hell, he felt incapable even of flexing his fingers inside the buckskin gloves.

For stretched seconds it seemed that only the hair on the nape of his neck was able to move, prickled as his ears filled with a roaring noise triggered by depthless fear that compounded toward terror. This as he realised that if he were truly deaf to sounds of danger and was paralysed against meeting it, he was totally helpless.

But somebody else experienced a similar level of fear.

A bone that cracked was not in Steele's petrified body. And as he remained rigid for a part of a second more he knew that if he heard the small sound, his hearing was back to normal. And if that were so, then maybe every other function of his being operated normally now.

He took a final wide-angle view of the slow-moving line of Indians down in the brightly moonlit and deeply shadowed valley: their heads turned away from the timber stand where he was hidden, to focus attention on the building in back of the fallen-down fence a hundred feet away.

As he did so, he needed consciously to rid his racing mind of anger at himself for failing to see that one brave had broken away under cover of the gunbattle, to work his way up the hill and locate the sentry whose warning had been yelled from the trees on the high ground. Then there had been the greater error of not spotting just nine Shoshone remained in the line until . . .

He whirled and dropped into a crouch: reached his right hand through the slit seam of his pants leg. Hurled himself to the ground, rolled and drew the knife out of the boot sheath.

The brave had gotten to within a dozen feet of Steele before aching tension caused the bone in a leg or arm to crack. He had planned a silent kill, for when he pulled up short in mid-stride his right hand was high in the air. Fisted around the handle of a knife that would have plunged into Steele's back if realisation had not struck the Virginian ahead of the blade.

Now the lithely-built brave attired in a waistcoat, weapons belt and breechclouts was committed. And after the moment it took him to recover from the shock of discovery, he lunged forward. Brought down the knife as a low sound, perhaps a Shoshone curse, ripped from his thin-lipped mouth set in the hard line of a snarl.

Steele made it back up into a crouch, left hand raised to combat the brave's attack and right poised to launch a counter. He was suddenly drenched with sweat: had the inconsequential notion that it must be the stink of the Indian that filled his nostrils. Which, damnit, should have alerted him to the brave's presence earlier.

But earlier no longer mattered.

The brave was stooped over him, had fastened a powerful grip around the wrist of the Virginian's knife hand. An instant later, with a little frantic judgment and a massive quantity of dumb luck, he managed to fasten a similar hold around the wrist of the Shoshone's right hand.

137

Steele's entire frame juddered with the impact of the brave's fast flying arm slamming into his palm that became a fist. He was knocked off his haunches out on to his back and the full weight of the other man landed on top of him with a force that emptied his lungs of breath with an inordinately loud whooshing sound.

He felt weaker than he could ever recall. And although he seemed to devote every fibre of his being toward massing strength in his left hand which was grasping the brave's right wrist, his opponent wrenched free. While his own knife hand remained held against the ground in the grip of the Shoshone which seemed impossible to shake off.

He heard the brave's whoop of triumph, which convinced him he was about to die. Then, not for the first time in a life during which violent death had often threatened, he experienced the phenomenon of mind over matter. This just as the victory roar of the Shoshone was taken as a signal by the braves in the valley: who vented a barrage of warcries, loosed off a fussilade of gunfire.

He was not going to die on the side of this mountain valley. On account of yelling a warning of an Indian attack to a bunch of no good thieving road agents. Knowing that some of them, at least, were surely bound to survive. Keep possession of the Colt Hartford until they got somewhere the gold plate could be removed and sold for its precious metal value.

Why the hell had he once again risked his life for that damn rifle? When he had something of so much more value back in the Providence River Valley?

The brave, his right arm flung high again now, showed his teeth and the whites of his eyes in a grin of triumphant satisfaction as he tasted victory, relished the prospect of the gush of blood that would signal his coup at the instant his knife plunged into the flesh of the white man.

Steele knew he had no hope of being able to fasten another hold on the Shoshone's knife hand. Nor of tearing his own right hand free of the brave's grip.

So he attacked his attacker where every man is most vulnerable. Felt calmly sure of himself as he timed the move to the split second: waited until the brave rose up on one knee to gain more height and so greater distance over which to power the knife thrust. Then brought across his empty left hand.

He reached under and into the breechclouts between the parted thighs of the brave. Once again he forced every ounce of strength to his hand. Formed it into a claw, closed it, clutched and wrenched.

The brave vented a piercingly shrill scream. Loud enough so it blotted out of Steele's hearing the sounds of the gunbattle in the valley.

The knife kept coming down as the brave snatched his other hand away from its grip on the Virginian's wrist, reached toward the source of his agony. He was weakened and unbalanced by such a high degree of pain and Steele was able to jerk himself out from under the descending blade, which thudded uselessly into the ground where his back had been pressed.

The scream seemed to shriek an octave higher. And as Steele rose on to all fours he thought the Shoshone was perhaps giving vent to the brand of disappointment that is always hardest to endure: that which has to be faced while the taste of lost success is still sour in the mouth. In this case compounded by the certain knowledge that defeat was inevitably to be followed by death.

Then the brave flipped over on to his back, the knife left buried in the earth as he brought up his knees to fold himself double, both hands clutched at his crotch. And Steele felt something moist and sponge-like under his gloved left hand, which he pressed against the ground to ease himself up to his haunches.

There was time then, while the now groaning brave writhed helplessly in agony, for the Virginian to realise what had happened: just what it was under his hand, which he dragged over the pine needles on the ground to wipe off the mess.

In that moment of kill or be killed, Steele had been blessed with a degree of strength that had reached superhuman proportions. In his fear of death, the determination to escape it, he had unwittingly wrenched off the Shoshone that which made him a man.

The Virginian tasted bile, forced himself to swallow it. Felt its acid sear his throat as he moved forward on hands and knees, still wiping the gore off his gloved palm while his other hand gripped his knife so tightly his arm ached from fingertips to shoulder.

Down in the valley the gunfire had become sporadic. There was no longer any shouting. Up here on the fringe of the pines, the brave stopped moaning and craned his head around to look up at the man crouched beside him.

It was not possible in the moon-shadowed darkness to clearly see the expression on his raddled, pock-marked face. Pain, for certain. Maybe mixed in with shame he had failed to claim the life of this White Eyes while his brother braves fought and died in the valley below. Perhaps, too, a fleeting hatred for the man who had gained victory over him and was about to kill him. Then, Steele thought, a kind of gratitude to him that he was going to finish the fight: end the life of a man who was no longer a man.

The Shoshone made no attempt to defend himself, try to avoid the knife that swung and plunged into his throat. The sound of his dying was a gasp, then a gurgle as blood from his severed jugular flooded into his windpipe. He gagged on this, then it gushed out of his mouth to mix with the torrent that gouted from the wound as Steele yanked the knife out of the flesh.

Once again Steele used the pine needles that carpeted the ground, wiped the blood off the blade of the knife before he pushed it back into the boot sheath. He muttered as he stood up: 'You had balls, feller.'

The gunfire in the valley had been curtailed now. And when Steele moved to look down on the familiar scene, he saw all the Shoshone were dead or dying. Lay in various attitudes at the side of the old army post, unfeelingly inert or writhing in pain: some not more than a few paces beyond the point where the attack was launched, two sprawled over the fallen fence.

'Steele, hey Steele, you okay?'

Because of the way loud sounds echoed in the rocky valley, the Virginian was not able to recognise which of the white men had shouted.

The horse in the trees behind him gave a nervous whinny, like it had only now sensed the proximity of fresh death. Other sounds within the stand of pines were less obtrusive as Steele stooped, took the revolver out of the dead brave's weapons belt, checked its load and found just two unfired rounds in the six chambers of the worse-for-wear Colt.

Steele did not like having to use other men's guns. Particularly he did not like to use revolvers, especially so when they were old and ill cared for. He considered a man could only truly trust his own tried and tested weapon. But there were times when circumstances dictated a man must alter the basic premises of how he lived his life: never more so than when that life depended upon it.

He had not realised how far the struggle with the Shoshone brave had shifted from where it started. And now, when he returned to the place from where he could look down into the valley, he saw that maybe he would not need to use the Indian's revolver that was so ill cared for.

Because the overall familiar scene which had always altered in detail each time he looked upon it had changed yet again: three people were moving down there, not posing an immediate threat to him.

The heavily-built Thelma Cowley had reached the fallen-down fence on the south side of the stone building and was picking her way cautiously over the collapsed timber stakes between the prone bodies of two Shoshone. She was further hampered by the burden she carried in both arms held out in front of her: the limp, unmoving form of her daughter.

Behind her, to her left, was the short and fat Daryl who walked with his left leg dragging and his left hand clutching at the thigh: clearly trying to ease the pain and staunch the flow of blood from a wound. His right hand was fisted around the barrel of a rifle sloped to his shoulder, stock end jutting out in back of him.

Some way off along the valley to the east, the leanly-built Mel was closing with the three horses which had plainly been spooked into a bolt by another barrage of gunfire during which they were not hobbled.

Steele saw the missing man as Thelma Cowley and Daryl came to a halt midway between the fallen-down fence and the start of the upslope of the valley's southern flank. Ricky sat on the ground with his back against the south wall of the former army post. His head was tipped forward, chin on his chest, one shoulder lower than the other, hands on their backs at either side of him. Clearly he was dead and had been propped in a prominent position so Steele could witness this.

Now the Virginian glanced elsewhere, and saw all nine sprawled Shoshone were unmoving. Dead for sure, none of them playing possum. The once arrogantly over-confident road agents had suffered bad losses, but they would not have been affected enough to have made that kind of mistake.

'You hear me, Steele?'

It was the same voice as before. Daryl, of course. Sounding less demanding. A little breathless, perhaps because of the pain in his leg wound: or maybe from fear. Then it was plainly jangling nerves that triggered his shriek:

'Answer me, you friggin——'

But Thelma Cowley jerked her head around to snarl something at him, forced him to cut short his profane aggression. And next assumed an attitude of gazing fixedly up at the centre of the pines, spoke loud enough for her words to carry to Steele. But although her voice was raised she managed to convey a brand of genuine sincerity which, he thought, the ugly old fat woman was not accustomed to feeling and expressing.

'I might be talkin' to you, Mr Steele! Or I might be addressin' myself to a heathen savage. Maybe I'm even talkin' to a couple of corpses. But I'm gonna get it said.'

She paused, obviously waiting for a response. But if she made any reaction to not getting one, she was too far away from Steele to see or hear it. She went on:

'It's over for us. Like you can see, my little girl is dead. Ricky Willis got it, too. But the way I see things, if it hadn't been for you, the whole bunch of us would be in the Promised Land by now. Murdered in our sleep. So we owe you. And we're gonna pay what we owe. Just like I said before the heathen savages sprung the second fight on us.'

They had discussed what was going to happen, so there was no need for an instruction to be given and an acknowledgment made. Daryl stepped up alongside the fat woman and yelled:

'So here it is, Steele! The lousy rifle that means so damn much to you! Come on down and get it when you're ready!'

With undisguised reluctance in his attitude, he thrust the rifle into the air, then stooped to lean it against a rock so it showed clearly in the moonlight that was starting to become less bright as the first streaks of grey dawn began to stain the sky above the mountain ridges in the south east.

Mel had retrieved the now docile horses and was bringing them back.

Thelma Cowley turned to watch this, then returned to peering up at the stand of pines as Steele backed off a little into the trees. She called up to him:

'We're gonna leave as soon as we've mounted, Mr Steele. Get the hell away from here and from you. Try to pick up the pieces of the kinda life we planned. You wanna take exception to that, you better be ready to kill the rest of us. And risk gettin' killed yourself.'

The woman with her daughter and the young man with his wounded leg moved sluggishly back to the former army post. Waited for the other survivor to return with the horses.

Steele continued to hold his peace, the Shoshone's gun low at his side, while he watched the saddling of the animals. Then the blanket-wrapped bodies of Belle and Ricky were draped over two horses. And Thelma Cowley, Daryl and Mel mounted up. All three rode off without a backward glance.

And Adam Steele tried to think why he should do something to prevent this.

The reward Alvin Townsend had put up for the return of his wife's jewellery?

Because the Cowley women and the men had held up the stage he was riding on, put him to the trouble of tracking them up here into the mountains? Where he had to engage in mortal combat with a Shoshone he beat by ripping off the brave's balls?

On moral grounds that they were killers and thieves, he was a law abiding citizen?

As he saw them ride out of the valley none of these sparked a positive reaction within his conscience. So he went to get the gelding, led him by the reins out of the pines and down the valley slope. And as he moved among the dead Shoshone he saw all of them were as under-nourished and ill-clothed as the one he killed in the timber.

They had been in much worse shape than the men and women who held up the stage: had some cause to . . .

He abandoned this line of thinking as he retrieved his rifle, checked the cylinder and was not surprised to find every chamber held an expended shell case. He could serve only as the judge and jury to justify his own actions. And by the code of his new style of living, he held that nobody ever had any call to take the life of another, except in defence of his own. Also, if life were taken for any other purpose, it was not his duty to see the guilty ones paid the price for their crimes.

He tossed away the Shoshone brave's revolver. Thought for a while about making use of the old army post which, up close, had obviously been abandoned many years ago: maybe was even a relic of the days when California had been Spanish territory. But now he had gotten his rifle back and found his conscience was clear, he no longer felt he had gone a night without sleep. And with the sky lightening toward dawn he knew that soon he would not be so cold. Too, the lower he walked down the mountain, the warmer he would be. And, anyway, he already felt a warm glow just to be going back home.